SHAKE IT UP

J. KENNER

M&O

Shake It Up

by

J. Kenner

Turn Me On Copyright © 2018 by Julie Kenner

Release Me excerpt Copyright © 2012 by Julie Kenner (used by permission with Bantam Books)

Cover design by Covers by Rogenna

Cover image by Periwinkle Photography

ISBN: 978-1-940673-78-3

Published by Martini & Olive Books

v. 2018-4-27P-a

Chapter One

TAYLOR D'ANGELO GRIMACED as she handed over her debit card. It was the reloadable kind, and she filled it up from her savings account at the beginning of every month with the exact amount of her budgeted expenses. Then she crossed her fingers, lit a candle, and begged the god of all things financial to let her go one more month without a crisis.

This month, the gods were apparently pissed, because as soon as the cashier swiped that card, Taylor would be officially one-hundred and fifty dollars over her monthly budget.

All because of some jerk who threw a brick through the window of her battered but reliable Toyota Corolla.

Six years ago, she'd talked herself into buying

the shiny gray car in the back of the used car lot. Not a dealership. No, she'd gone to the kind of place that either took cash or used a guy named Guido for financing. It had taken her a solid afternoon to finally make up her mind, but she hadn't regretted the decision. The car was plain, with no bells or whistles, but it was hers. And it represented freedom.

That was one of the few times she'd used the money she got from her dad. As far as she was concerned, it was blood money. For years, she'd tried to pretend the money wasn't there. But then college rolled around, and she'd had to make a hard decision—postpone school so that she could work and save tuition money, or enroll and use those tainted dollars for something good.

She'd enrolled. And she'd used the money for her first semester's tuition and for the deposit on her apartment.

By sophomore year, she'd racked up decent grades, and managed to score some scholarships. Between that money and her small work-study salary, she was holding her own. Her father's money could rot in the bank, for all she cared.

For that matter, now that she was close to

getting her masters, she could easily donate all that was left to charity.

Except she didn't. She wouldn't. Because someday she might need it again. Not for an education, but for survival.

Someday, she might have to run.

Please, God, no. Let it be over. Let me be safe.

Across the counter, the register spit out a receipt, accompanied by an electronic chirp that pulled Taylor from her thoughts. The cashier slid the receipt toward her, and for just a minute, Taylor hesitated. It would be so easy to use her stash to cover the deductible. To get ahead of the rent and the groceries. Would that really be so bad?

Yeah. Yeah, it really would.

Taylor sighed, the pen loose in her hand.

"Something wrong?" The girl behind the counter had perfect skin, perfectly manicured nails, perfectly styled blonde hair, and probably a perfect life to go with it, not to mention parents who were not only paying her way through college, but actually loved her.

Bitter much?

Taylor shook her head. "No. No problem. It's just been a crappy week. The expensive kind."

"I hear you. I was supposed to go to San

Antonio with some friends, but I'm a little short on rent, so I grabbed an extra shift." She waved her hand to indicate the interior of the auto-glass repair shop. A man in a suit sat reading a trade journal. A guy in biker boots and beady eyes cleaned under his nails with the tip of a pocket knife. "But that's okay. The fun never stops here."

Taylor laughed, feeling like a total bitch for her earlier catty thoughts. She wasn't usually so judgy. After all, she knew better than anyone that what you saw on the outside rarely matched a person's inside.

She signed the slip, then slid it back to the cashier, who traded it for her keys.

Her car was behind the shop, and as soon as she was in it, she closed her eyes and told herself she'd done the right thing and everything was good. That was true, and she knew it. She was just so tired of being broke. Because honestly, doing the right thing paid for shit.

Still, she was getting by. She had a great job with Texas Performing Arts as part of a work-study program, and that took the edge off. It didn't pay much, but the experience was invaluable. She'd been doing the job since her sophomore year, and now she was close to graduating with her master's degree. So she tended to get the plum assignments based on seniority alone.

Plus, she was getting paid to stage manage the Man of the Month contest at The Fix on Sixth, and that was fun, quick work for decent money. The calendar contest had been conceived to bring more traffic to The Fix a few months ago when the bar was having some serious financial trouble. It had gone over even better than anticipated, and now the bar was drawing impressive crowds every night, not only on the bi-weekly Wednesdays when the contest was held.

She checked her watch, saw that it was three hours to showtime, and cursed. She liked to have a full three hours for prep, and now tonight was going to be tight.

Frustrated, she turned the key. The car rattled to life, and she pulled out into the five o'clock traffic that was clogging Burnet Road, then navigated south toward The Fix.

With traffic, it took her almost forty-five minutes to get downtown, find a parking space that didn't cost more than her rent, then sprint to The Fix. She burst breathless through the doors, only to find that someone had already wheeled the spotlight out of the storage closet and set it up exactly how she liked it.

She detoured right toward the bar instead of left toward the stage, then squeezed in beside Jenna, one of the co-owners of The Fix and the woman in charge of the contest. "Did you do that?"

Jenna tucked a strand of long, red hair behind her ear as she shook her head.

Before Taylor could ask who did, Cameron Reed slid down the bar with a Diet Coke for her. "When Mina realized you were running late, she thought she'd help out."

"I appreciate it," Taylor said. Mina was Cameron's girlfriend, and she'd recently graduated from the University with her master's in film. "Of course, I'd appreciate it more if you'd put a little rum in this." She shook the ice in her glass. "It's been a crazy day."

"What's going on?" Jenna asked.

"Nothing that shining a spotlight on twelve guys as they strip off their shirts and walk across the stage won't fix."

Jenna laughed, and Taylor tossed a grin toward Cam, with his broad shoulders and ocean blue eyes. "We have quite a few calendar alumni working here. Maybe we should make them all go shirtless."

"I'm gonna vote no on that," Cam—Mr. March —said. "And I'm guessing Reece and Tyree would, too."

"I'll veto it," Jenna said, her hand on her belly even though her pregnancy had yet to show. "As far as I'm concerned, except for his calendar photo and those few minutes on stage, no one sees Reece shirt-less but me."

Taylor laughed, but Cam was holding up the soda gun and using it as a pointer as he said, "I almost forgot. Taylor, someone left a note for you. I put it in the office. Give me a sec and I'll go get it." He moved back down the bar, leaving Eric Shay, the other bartender working the main bar tonight, in charge.

Taylor watched, the back of her neck prickling, as Cam disappeared into the short hallway that led to the bar's back office. She took a sip of Diet Coke, telling herself this was no big deal. Just like the first note had been no big deal.

But still, she couldn't shake the sensation of dread.

About two weeks ago, she'd found an anony-mous greeting card inside her backpack. It must have been shoved in at some point when she was in the drama department. She'd changed backpacks

7

that morning, and when the pack wasn't on the floor in the theater's scene shop—a cavernous room where the sets were built—

it had been on her shoulder or in the trunk of her car, so there was no other possibility.

She'd found the envelope late that night when she was pulling out all of her junk so that she could settle in at her kitchen table and get some work done. It was tucked in between two scripts and a bound collection of classic farces that she needed to read. Her name glared at her in blue ink, the stylized letters taking up most of the envelope, and she'd assumed it was an invitation to an after-show party.

Inside, an old-fashioned style greeting card featured a window with gossamer curtains flowing in a breeze. The inscription on the inside of card read, *Even now, I'm at your window.*

Which, of course, would be creepy if Taylor hadn't understood the reference—a line from a song featured in the musical *Sweeney Todd*. The musical reference had made her certain that Reggie had left it.

A senior in the department, Reggie Jones was one of fifteen underclassmen in Dr. Bishop's seminar class on scene design. Taylor wasn't formally working as Bishop's teaching assistant, but he was her graduate advisor, and when he'd asked her to give a presentation on minimalistic design, she'd eagerly done so.

Afterwards, Reggie had been one of the students who'd hung around to talk shop, and when she'd bumped into him later in the common area, they'd chatted about their shared love of musical theater, and of Sondheim's work in particular.

Two casual encounters later, and he confessed that he was working up the courage to ask her out.

She'd turned him down, of course. For one thing, she wasn't attracted to him at all. But since that wasn't the kind of thing you told a guy, she'd simply said that she wasn't dating. That there just wasn't time for a relationship.

All true, just not the entire truth. She had no interest in getting into a relationship, and her life was far too complicated to date, though she wasn't averse to the occasional hook-up. But not with Reggie. Not with any guy who might want to stick.

"Taylor?" Startled, she jerked her head up to Jenna, then realized she'd been staring at the bubbles in her drink, probably looking hypnotized. "What? Oh, sorry. I was zoning. I'm fine." She smiled brightly, and forced her mood to match her appearance.

But as soon as Cam returned with the note, her facade collapsed. The envelope was the same. The size of a greeting card. High quality paper, and her name in stylized handwriting. She swallowed. Probably still Reggie. He knew she worked here. He probably thought he was being cute, wooing her with cards. He probably had a whole campaign planned out. Card after card, and then he'd send one attached to roses, and ask her out again.

It had to be Reggie. Because, dammit, the alternative just wasn't something she was prepared to think about.

Slowly, she slid her finger under the flap and loosened the glue. Then she pried it up, and carefully tugged out the card. A closed pair of eyes on the cover. Inside the card, someone had written, *You belong to me.*

The card tumbled from her hand, and she licked her lips. "Hey, Cam?" Her voice, she noticed, sounded so normal. "Did you see who left this?"

"Sorry. It was last night. We were swamped, and I was covering for Eric, so it was just me back here."

"Right. Sure." She cleared her throat. "Do you remember if it was a guy with really yellow hair.

Kinda messy?" Maybe it really was Reggie. After all, *Phantom of the Opera* had a song that fit. *Close your eyes*, the Phantom sang to Christina. And then later, *you belong to me.*

Not Sondheim, but still musical theater.

Cam shook his head. "Sorry. Doesn't ring a bell."

Jenna pressed her hand over Taylor's. "You're freaking me out. What's going on? Who's got yellow hair?"

Taylor tried to shrug it off. "Just a guy at school. He's got an aggressive crush." She lifted a shoulder. "And I'm really not interested."

She could tell that Jenna wasn't convinced, and before the other woman could push the issue, Taylor glanced down at Jenna's still-flat belly. "I'm so glad the baby's okay. I'm so, so sorry."

"Are you kidding?" Jenna's hand went protectively over her belly. "It wasn't your fault at all. We're fine. And I'm the one who's sorry. I mean, your car. You're going to send me the bill for the windshield, right?"

"Don't be silly. Insurance totally covered it." A lie, but she wasn't about to make Jenna feel any worse than she already did, even if repayment would add a hundred and fifty bucks back into

Taylor's dwindling account. "Besides, it could just as easily have happened to me. I mean if I'd been—"

Of course. How could she have been so stupid?

That brick wasn't random, and it damn sure hadn't been meant for Jenna. It had been a warning for Taylor.

She looked down, then realized she'd crumpled the card into a ball, and now her hand was fisted tightly around it.

Not Reggie. Of course, it hadn't been Reggie.

He'd found her. Somehow, he'd found her.

"Okay, Taylor, I'm sorry, but you're starting to freak me out."

"What? Why?"

"Are you coming down with something?" Jenna reached out and felt Taylor's forehead, and Taylor almost laughed.

"You'll make a good mom."

"And you make a lousy patient." She lifted her hand, signaling for someone behind Taylor to come over.

"What's up?" Mina asked, scooting between the two of them and hooking her arms around their shoulders. She wore her hair in a pixie cut and grinned impishly at both of them before blowing a kiss at Cam.

"I'm sending Taylor home," Jenna said. "She's coming down with something. Can you play stage manager for the night?"

"Oh, like what I do is just a game," Taylor quipped.

Mina stood up straight so she could rub her hands together. "I totally can. I'll just aim the spot at whoever's the hottest, and—"

"Yeah, yeah," Jenna said. "If I let you do that, you'd just keep it aimed over the bar on Cam."

"Not a chance," Mina retorted, as Cam squared his shoulders and buffed his nails on his chest. "I don't want to point him out to the rest of the world any more than necessary. You're mine," she added to Cam.

"Wouldn't have it any other way."

The women laughed. "Good answer," Mina said.

"You sure you don't mind?" Taylor focused her attention on Mina. "I really do feel off today."

"Are you kidding? It'll be fun."

"Thanks." She slid off the stool, leaving a bill for the soda and a tip. "I'm gonna get out of here before it gets crazy busy."

Since it was early August, the sun hadn't set yet, though it was dipping low in the sky behind her, casting long shadows in front as she walked east along Sixth Street toward the parking lot. She kept her eyes on the shadow, only realizing how jumpy she was whenever another shadow encroached, indicating someone moving up fast behind her.

Twice, she whipped around to see who was walking, only to end up startling a man in a business suit, and a tall girl in jeans and a tank top who was bopping along to the sound of her earbuds.

"Chill," she ordered herself, then jumped a mile when the chirp of her cell phone signaled an incoming text. She cursed her nerves again, opened the text, and froze.

It was a picture of herself leaving her apartment, decked out in skinny jeans and a *Phantom of the Opera* touring company T-shirt, her long brown hair hanging loose around her shoulders on one of the rare days when she hadn't pulled it back. *Yesterday*.

She stood there, waiting for another text. A message. An emoji. Anything to tell her what this meant. Or to tell her for certain who it came from.

Except she already knew the answer to that question. Didn't she?

And if she was right, she had only two choices: Run. Or get help.

She thought about starting over. About the logistics of finding a safe place to hide. About being alone without her friends. Without a job. With absolutely nothing except her wits. And, of course, her father's money.

A shudder cut through her, and she knew what she had to do.

She turned around, and one step at a time, she started walking back down Sixth Street toward The Fix.

Chapter Two

TAYLOR PAUSED OUTSIDE THE FIX, still uncertain. But what choice did she have? She could either run, or she could get help. And—

"Taylor!"

She turned, to see Megan Clark behind her. A makeup artist by trade, Megan had recently started working at The Fix to make some extra money. A fact that reminded Taylor that she could surely do the same if the new hole in her bank account made it necessary.

"Why aren't you in there? Aren't you working today?" Megan asked.

"Mina's covering for me. I'm feeling crappy so Jenna sent me home. But I really need to talk to Brent, so I thought I'd grab him before I go megadose on NyQuil and crash." As soon as the words were out, she regretted them. Megan would want to know what was so important it had Taylor running to Brent. Not because she was inherently nosy, but because they'd become good friends. And good friends talked.

She cleared her throat, then rushed on before Megan could get any reply in. "Are we running this weekend?" Megan, Mina, and Taylor had started training together for a 5K, with the ultimate goal of running in the Capitol 10K next year. A goal they probably wouldn't reach since most of their running sessions turned into too-short runs and too-long breakfasts.

A couple circled them, then pulled the door open.

"We're blocking traffic." Megan shoved her cat's eye glasses up her nose, then reached for the door as it closed behind the couple. "And yes," she said, holding it open for Taylor. "Absolutely we're running. And after, there's this new place that's supposed to do amazing Tex-Mex breakfasts. We should check it out."

Taylor bit back a smile, amused by how well the conversation was tracking her own thoughts. "Sounds good," she said, then stepped inside. Immediately, the noise surrounded her. The familiar, constant din of a bar full of carefree people who'd come to have some fun. "I'm going to go find Parker," Megan said, referring to her ultra-sexy boyfriend. "I was supposed to have met him five minutes ago. *Oh.* There's Brent."

Taylor followed Megan's finger to the back, told her friend she'd catch up with her later, then wove her way through the crowd until she reached Brent, who was standing by both Tyree and Reece. *Great.* So much for keeping this on the down low.

"I thought Jenna sent you home," Reece said in lieu of a greeting as Taylor approached.

"She did. I needed to come back." Taylor looked between the three of them, working up the courage to pull Brent aside and spill all of her woes. She knew she needed to, and the sooner the better. Already she felt calmer, just standing near the three.

And why not? She was awash in a sea of testosterone. And she was certain that any one of the three would help her if she asked and protect her if she needed. They were just those kind of guys. Reece, the bar's manager, with his stellar body covered with intricate tats, and the shaved head and beard he rocked so perfectly. Tyree—the original owner and founder of The Fix—who stood like a grizzly of a man, exuding both strength and patience. And Brent, a former cop and single dad who ran security for the bar. He was the only one of the three who hadn't been anointed as a Man of the Month, although Taylor happened to know that wasn't for lack of trying. Jenna was forever harassing him to enter, and lately Megan had jumped on that bandwagon, too.

Taylor figured they'd win that battle eventually. And when they did, Brent would win the contest. He had the kind of good looks Hollywood casting agents rubber-stamped with *Leading Man*. And the best part about Brent was that he didn't even seem to realize it. He focused on his job, his daughter, and his friends.

Today, Taylor really hoped she ranked in that last category, because his help was the reason she'd come back.

"—okay?"

She shook her head to clear it, then realized she'd only heard half of what Reece had said. "I'm sorry. What?"

"I said, hurry and get whatever you came back for, then get out of here. Trust me."

"He means that Jenna is in full-on mother hen mode," Brent said, chuckling. "If she sent you home, she wants you home."

"Got it," Taylor said. "But could I talk to you first?"

Brent's whiskey-brown eyes widened. "Well, sure. But the contest—"

"I know," she said. "But it's important. It's, um, a security thing."

At that, he shifted from laid-back to all-business. "We can talk in Tyree's office. I'll catch you guys later," he added to the other two, who, to Taylor's relief, didn't ask a single question.

As soon as she'd crossed over the threshold, she shut the door behind her. Brent noticed, but said nothing, just nodded to the guest chair in front of Tyree's desk. She sat, expecting him to sit in Tyree's chair. Instead, he leaned against the desk, his brow furrowed with concern. "So what's going on?"

"It's not about The Fix," she said quickly. "I'm sorry if you thought there was some sort of crisis on the job. There's not. Or, I guess, if there is, I don't know about it." She wanted to spit everything out. Instead she was rambling. Why was this so difficult?

Except that was a ridiculous question; she knew damn well why it was difficult. Because she'd been self-reliant for so long that getting help almost felt like she was breaking a secret pact she'd made with herself all those years ago. In a way, she supposed she was. But things had changed, and she loved this life. And, dammit, she wasn't going to give it up without a fight.

"It might be easier if you close your eyes," Brent said gently.

A laugh burbled out of her. "Is that what you tell Faith?" she asked, referring to his five-year-old daughter.

"Sometimes. It works."

She shook her head. "I'm okay. It's just hard figuring out where to start."

"Start with what brought you here. Then you can go backwards."

"I'm being stalked." There. She'd said it.

In front of her, Brent's face remained exactly the same, and she thought that he must have made a damn good cop if he could sit across from a witness or a suspect and not react at all. "You're sure?"

She nodded.

"Tell me what's happened."

She passed him the crumpled note that she'd shoved into the leather messenger bag she used as a purse. "Someone left that for me on the bar. Cam found it yesterday and gave it to me just a bit ago."

He took the note carefully, then moved around

the desk to unfold it, using a tissue so that his fingers didn't directly touch it.

She grimaced. "I didn't think about messing up fingerprints. And I left the envelope on the bar. It's probably buried under a mountain of old food and yucky napkins."

"I doubt there are prints anyway, but I prefer to be careful." He continued what he was doing, then frowned when he saw the words.

"You belong to me," he quoted, then looked up. "Do you know who sent it?"

"Maybe," she said, then explained about the other note with the quote from *Sweeney Todd* and how the note he was holding might be a reference to *The Phantom of the Opera*. "There's a guy in my department at school who's been asking me out. But I just don't think he's the type to take pictures of me or throw bricks." She shuddered, once again thinking about what could have happened to Jenna. She'd lost control of the car, but the damage to the car had been minor. Crunched metal, but nothing that affected how the car drove. And Taylor could live with a bumped and bruised Corolla.

"Tell me about the picture."

Obediently, she passed him her phone, open to the text message.

"You're wearing a *Phantom* T-shirt. You might be right about the student."

"Maybe." She hoped she was. A scary Reggie was a lot less scary than the alternative. "I don't know. He's so … mild," she finished lamely.

"Still waters," Brent said. "And if he has psychopathic tendencies … well, you just never know what he might be capable of."

She nodded, feeling both numb and oddly better. She was doing something, and action felt good. "So you think it might not be out of character for him to have thrown the brick?"

"I'm not sure he did throw it. Three other cars had bricks thrown through their windows that week. The police have been searching footage from nearby cameras, but so far, no leads on who did it."

"Really?" She sat back in her chair, relieved that it was looking less and less that her past was coming back to haunt her. Still, she wasn't too keen on being stalked in her present. "So what should I do?"

"Well, you're not staying at home tonight. Not until we get you some decent security at your apartment."

She nodded, thinking about how much *that* was going to cost.

"And I'm going to talk to Landon."

At the name, Taylor felt something warm and reassuring flow through her. She didn't know Landon well, but she trusted him. A gorgeous black man with kind eyes, a close-shaved scalp and beard, and a full lower lip, she'd first noticed Landon when she'd bumped into him—literally—at the entrance to The Fix.

That had been mortifying—she'd been such a klutz. And despite the fact that the feel of those hard muscles had definitely resonated, she'd put the memory aside. At least until the next time Landon had caught her eye. He'd been at The Fix with Derek Winston, the heir to a hotel chain and one of tonight's contestants for Mr. July.

Then again, *caught her eye* wasn't entirely accurate. More like *captured her with his intense, heated gaze.*

That night, Landon and Derek had been sitting at the bar, and she'd been sitting with Mina and Megan just a few feet away at one of the tables by the windows. He'd turned, their eyes had locked, and *zing*—Taylor had felt the shock of his gaze running all the way through her, heating every part of her body all the way down to her toes—and more interesting parts in between.

They hadn't said a word, but that was the moment that Landon had become her unreasonable crush and her favorite bedtime fantasy, with his perfect ass and broad shoulders taking second billing to all the wonderful things that gorgeous mouth could do to her.

Then the full scope of what Brent was suggesting hit her, and Taylor shook her head. "I can't," she blurted. "I don't want to go to the police."

Brent's brows furrowed, because obviously any sane person would be happy to go to the police. Taylor, however, did not. "He's on leave, actually. Three weeks. Take it or lose it vacation, so he took off to do some work on his house."

"Oh. It's just—"

He moved closer, so that he was right in front of her, his eyes on hers. "I know the idea of going to the police makes people nervous, so I'm giving you a pass on that with the caveat that you file a report if anything more happens. *And* with the caveat that you let Landon help you."

"Can't you?"

He shook his head. "I've got too much on my plate right now. Landon painting and redoing floors, but he's tackling it slowly."

"Still, that's time-consuming. And I doubt he wants to play detective when he's on vacation from that very job." She needed to shut up, and she knew it. There was no reason to turn down Landon's help, and the only reason she was hesitating was the fact that she was attracted to him.

The corner of Brent's mouth quirked up, and she had the uncomfortable feeling that he'd read her mind. "He'll want to help you. I'm sure of it. And, hell. Maybe you can help him paint his house."

She drew in a breath, then slowly released it. "Okay. Sounds good. Thank you."

He nodded. "I'll give him a call in a bit. In the meantime, you can stay at my place tonight."

"Oh, no." She shook her head vehemently. "It'll probably all be fine, but if something bad did happen—I mean, with Faith there." She met his eyes. "No. Thank you, but no way."

For a moment, he just held her gaze. "Is there something you haven't told me?"

A chill raced down her spine. "No," she lied. "I just—she's a little girl, and I'd feel horrible if…"

She trailed off, and he nodded. "Fair enough," Brent said. "We'll get you a room at The Winston. Since Derek's about to strut his stuff across stage, I'll get Reece to check you in, and I'll tell Derek as soon as he's done with the contest. He can give a heads-up to hotel security so they can keep an eye on your room. Just in case."

"Okay." She forced herself not to think about the dollars that were stacking up. "And Landon? I mean, Detective Ware?"

"I think Landon works just fine. I'll talk with him and explain the situation. I'll have him come by to see you in the morning. And I'll send Mina over later tonight so you have some company. Okay?"

She nodded as he checked his phone, then confirmed he had her cell number.

"You ready? We can go track down Reece and get you settled."

For just a moment, she hesitated. She didn't like being a burden. More than that, she didn't like being under a microscope. Too many secrets that had the potential of coming out.

But she also didn't like the idea of ending up dead. Or worse.

"Yeah," she said. "I'm ready."

Chapter Three

"YO, WARE!" Matthew Herrington's voice echoed across the cavernous gym to where Detective Landon Ware was beating the shit out of a punching bag since he couldn't take his fists to Terrance Weems, a scumbag Landon had put away a year ago, and the system had kicked back out on parole. First thing Terrance did was go home and knock out his ex-wife's front teeth.

He was back in the pen, and he'd probably stay this time, but dammit, Landon had busted his ass to get the shithead locked up. To protect that poor woman whom Weems had spent years waling on. And one idiotic bureaucratic decision had destroyed all of that.

He loved his job, dammit. But there were times when the system was seriously fucked up.

"Your cell phone's ringing. Display says it's from Brent Sinclair. Want me to answer?"

"Just let it roll to voice mail," Landon said. He'd see Brent soon enough. Tonight Landon's buddy Derek was running the Man of the Month gauntlet at The Fix, just a couple of blocks away from Herrington's gym. That's what came from being in love. Derek's girlfriend was Amanda, and Amanda's best friend was in charge of the contest. Which meant that when one of the contestants had to drop out, she'd tagged Derek.

Landon assumed that Amanda had encouraged him to do it and would undoubtedly be yelling the loudest when Derek stripped off his shirt. They were a good match, Landon would give them that. But good matches were rare in his experience, and he hoped his friend appreciated what he had.

Then again, Derek had been topsy-turvy for Amanda for a while now, and the fact that she was finally all-in had Derek doing a permanent happy dance.

Which, of course, explained why Derek had agreed to do the contest. And why Landon was heading to The Fix next, just to watch his friend's abject humiliation. Or rather, that was where he was heading after he'd burned off enough of his bad mood to be decent company.

He kept at it for another ten minutes, and by the time he stopped, his arms felt like spaghetti. "Not a bad workout," Matthew said. "Good thing I only invest in quality gym equipment. Pretty sure you would have come near to destroying another bag."

Matthew wasn't wrong, but there was humor in his voice.

"I was picturing a particular face," Landon admitted.

"Rough day at the office?"

"The roughest," Landon said. "Which says a lot considering I'm on vacation."

"Did it help?" Matt nodded toward the punching bag.

Landon tried out a smile, managed a slight grin. "Guess so. At least a little."

"Then I'm happy to have been of service. You heading to The Fix?"

Landon nodded. "As soon as I shower. You?"

"I shouldn't, but I am."

"Shouldn't?" Landon had been mopping his face with one of the chilled towels that Matthew kept in three small refrigerators around the gym.

Now he peered at his friend. "Why not? I know you're not giving up whiskey. Selma would disown you."

Matthew and Landon had met in high school, where their favorite occupations were running track and teasing Selma, Matthew's quirky sister, who now ran a local distillery that was gaining national attention.

"Nah, nothing like that," Matthew said. "It's just that there's this woman who hangs out there sometimes. This lawyer, and she's, well, it doesn't matter..." He trailed off with a shrug, and Landon sighed. He considered diving into part two of his lecture about how Matthew needed to get over the fact that he'd dropped out of high school. He'd opened a successful chain of gyms, had a full-to-overflowing bank account, and was a genuinely nice guy. Any woman who couldn't see that was an idiot.

Not that Matthew lacked for female companionship. As a gym owner, it was part of his job to stay in shape, and Landon had noticed that Matthew rarely lacked a woman on his arm. Or, presumably, in his bed. That, apparently, wasn't enough to quiet the self-doubt. Which, Landon thought, was a damn shame, because Matthew actually wanted a relationship. Wanted to wake up next to a woman, and go to bed with her every night. A lover. A friend.

A wife.

And, dammit, Landon didn't have the heart to tell his friend that what he wanted was a goddamn fantasy. *For better or for worse* was bullshit except for those few lucky ones. He thought Derek and Amanda fit that bill. He hoped they did. But the odds were good that Matthew wouldn't get that lucky.

God knew, Landon himself had played the odds, only to have fate give him a swift, hard kick in the balls.

Determined not to bring Matthew down, Landon forced the thoughts of Vanessa from his mind. "Let me grab a shower and we can walk over together. You got someone watching the desk?"

Matthew shook his head. "I changed up the hours. Gold members only after seven-thirty. By then, the after-work crowd's cleared out, and everyone who's gold has a key fob to get in."

Landon nodded, then headed back to the locker room. The Lavaca Street location of Herrington's Gym was one of six in the Austin metropolitan area, and Matthew was talking to an attorney about franchising his business. Landon hoped it worked out; from what he'd seen, Matthew was making bank. Apparently there were a lot of people out there willing to pay good money to sweat, himself included.

Fifteen minutes later, though, that sweat had been showered away, and he was clean and dressed in jeans, boots, and a clean Austin Police Department T-shirt. The walk to The Fix was short—just a few blocks to the north on Congress, and then a few blocks to the east on Sixth—and they arrived with fifteen minutes to spare, to find there wasn't a seat left in the house.

They parted ways, Landon to go track down Brent, and Matthew to try to wrangle a free chair, though Landon was pretty sure his real plan was reconnaissance in the hopes of finding the lawyer he was so interested in. As for himself, Landon found Brent near the back, lecturing a skinny-ass kid who'd apparently tried to buy whiskey using a fake ID.

As soon as the kid scurried off toward the exit, Landon met Brent's eyes. His friend shook his head, half-amused, half-exasperated. "Kids," Brent said.

"Rough gig you got here," Landon said. "Sure you don't want to come back to the APD?"

"Don't be an asshole," Brent shot back. "You

know damn well I miss it. You also know why I left."

"Sorry, you're right," Landon said, feeling chastised. "I'm just being an ass." After all, he *did* know why Brent walked away from the department almost six years ago, despite having just made lieutenant. Not only that, but Landon knew that Brent genuinely loved his job, and The Fix, and the people he worked with. "It's been a rough day."

"Come work with me," Brent suggested. "You just saw about how rough my world gets lately." He spread his hands. "But at least I know my little girl has a parent coming home every night."

Since any discussion of the inherent dangers of the job inevitably reminded Landon of why Vanessa left, he shifted the subject back on topic. "I saw you called. Checking to see if I was coming tonight?"

"Hell, yeah. Didn't you know it's my life's mission to keep tabs on you?"

Landon shook his head. "Funny."

"No, the truth is, I need a favor."

"Anything, man. You know that." As he spoke, the now-familiar Man of the Month music filled the bar, and the spotlight caught Beverly Martin, a rising indie film star who was the contest's emcee, as she walked up the stairs. Almost out of reflex, Landon craned his neck, looking not at Beverly, but off stage to the spot operator. He expected to see Taylor. Hell, he *wanted* to see her.

Instead, Mina was there.

Before he could check himself, he'd whipped back around to face Brent. "Where's Taylor?" he asked, and although it might have been his imagination, he was pretty sure he saw a flicker of amusement play over Brent's face.

"And that, my friend, is the favor."

TAYLOR.

Someone was stalking Taylor.

And dear God, if that sonofabitch laid so much as a finger on her, Landon would rearrange his face and teach him a new definition of pain.

He drew in a breath, trying to force himself back down to calm.

Shit.

Too bad *calm* was proving to be more than a little difficult to reach. He had to settle for taking slow, measured breaths. His mind was still churning, but his body relaxed. The calm before the storm, maybe. But at least it was one brand of calm.

Landon and Brent had moved into Tyree's office, and now that Landon was replaying the highlights of their conversation over again in his mind, it was taking every ounce of his concentration to keep his shit together. Especially when all he really wanted to do was put his fist through a wall. Or, better, through the asshole student who'd been stalking her.

Assuming it was the asshole student.

"What else do you know about this kid? Do we have a name?"

"*We* don't. But if you're willing to step in and keep an eye on her, I'm sure you can get her to tell you."

"I want to know if he has a record. If anyone at the University has filed a harassment claim. Talk to some of his classmates. See if any of them have the vibe."

"Which means you're going to do this," Brent said, the words a statement, not a question.

"Yeah," Landon said, without missing a beat. "I'm going to do this." The truth was, he barely knew Taylor, but the woman had gotten under his skin. He'd first seen her when she'd crashed into him on the sidewalk just outside The Fix. He'd been coming out; she'd been racing to get there on time. Her body and been flush against his for a few seconds, and in that short amount of time, he'd pretty much seen heaven.

She'd mumbled flustered apologies and disappeared inside, leaving him to his prurient fantasies.

A few weeks later, he'd popped into The Fix to watch the Man of the Month contest after Brent had given him a heads-up, and he'd been curious enough to take a look.

He'd been glad that he had. Not because he gave a flip about the men strutting around on that stage, but because he'd sat in the back of the bar, his view of the stage partially blocked by the same woman. He got a better look at her that time. A dark-haired woman with a ponytail, the kind of small waist a man could use for a handhold, and the biggest brown eyes he'd ever seen.

But it was her face that had really done him in. Pretty, but not classically so. Her mouth was a little too wide, her nose a little too crooked, her chin just slightly off center. But those brilliant eyes ... damn, but they could light up a room.

As far as Landon was concerned, it was the most interesting face he'd ever seen, and it was paired with a body that had conjured the kind of thoughts that made his mouth go dry. She'd been leaning forward over a step stool as she operated the spotlight, and he'd had a truly enticing view of thighs, long and lean and undoubtedly strong enough to wrap tight around a man.

He'd lost all interest in the contest at that moment, and he'd spent the time watching the girl. The way her small, cute ass moved in her jeans. The smile that lit her face when she turned and greeted a friend.

Holy hell, she'd gotten under his skin. And he'd been back every contest since. Sometimes just sitting in the back, alone and anonymous. Other times chatting with Brent or Derek. On more than one occasion, he'd caught her eye across the bar and felt the sparks fly between them.

He'd learned her name, of course, and they'd even spoken a few times, her melodic voice dancing over his body in a way that made him want to run back to Herrington's Gym and take a cold shower.

She'd told him that she was a graduate student in the theater department who Jenna had hired as a stage manager. And each time he came to watch the contest, he'd expected her to be less enticing. That he'd look at her and simply see a pretty white woman. Not someone who made his body fire simply from the sight of her.

Yet that reaction never faded. If anything it had grown stronger.

He knew better than to think that meant anything, of course. There'd been only one other woman in his life with whom he'd felt that kind of instant attraction—*Vanessa*. And God knew that hadn't turned out well.

On top of that, Taylor had to be at least ten years younger than him, and as far as Landon was concerned, that was too damn young.

The girl was off-limits. No two ways about it.

But goddammit, he couldn't stay away. Especially not now that he knew someone was harassing her.

On the contrary, he'd stick to her like glue.

He'd protect her.

That was all he *could* do, and he told himself it would be enough for her.

But it damn sure wouldn't be enough for him.

He shifted in the chair, turning his attention back to Brent, who was looking at him with the kind of expression that suggested he could read Landon's mind. "Where is she?" he asked.

"I put her up at The Winston," Brent said. "I

talked to Derek before the contest, and he called his security people. They'll keep an eye on the room, and she's registered under my name."

"Good."

"I told Mina to go by after the contest. I wasn't sure when I'd get in touch with you, and I figured she'd want a friend there tonight. I suggested she take a bottle of wine, order a movie, and the two of them should just kick back and forget about the whole thing."

Again, Landon nodded. "Also good." He didn't need to go tonight. Better to give her a chance to rest. To gather her thoughts. To have one last night before she was shadowed by a cop.

Definitely best for her if he went by first thing in the morning.

The hell of it was, though, Landon didn't want to wait.

Chapter Four

AS FAR AS Taylor was concerned, The Winston Hotel was the absolute best ever. Sure, the room was small—just one room with a king-size bed, a small sofa, and a wall unit with drawers and a desk —but there was a television with access to the internet, and the bathroom had a steam shower and a wonderfully deep tub.

Heaven.

The manager had actually apologized for not having a larger room for "Mr. Winston's guest," then went on to explain to her and Reece how they were almost at full capacity, and that she had literally been booked into the last available room.

She'd nodded and smiled and told him that she didn't care, but he'd apologized profusely all the way to the room. He'd personally walked her and

Reece there, then reviewed the room's amenities, which included a small hidden fridge, a coffee maker, and a complimentary bathrobe. And, since he'd apparently been forewarned that this was an unexpected trip for her, he'd also supplied her with a Winston Hotels logo tote bag with a toothbrush, a razor, deodorant, a hairbrush, a bar of chocolate, a charging cord for her phone, and a Winston Hotels t-shirt.

Considering she was being harassed by a potentially nutso stalker, it was all pretty cool.

As for the room, she didn't care that it was small. It wasn't as if she was going to be throwing parties or having guests over.

The manager had left her with his card and a promise that security would be doing regular passes by her room, and a reminder that this floor could be accessed only with a keycard. "We'll take good care of you, Ms. D'Angelo," he'd said before leaving, and she wasn't sure if that made her feel better —or if all his words did was reinforce that she was walking around with a target on her back.

The latter, she decided, after Reece reminded her that she shouldn't leave the room, then asked if she wanted him to stay for a while.

She'd assured him she was fine, but the way

he'd studied her with those cool, observant eyes only reminded her that she was in a hotel not because she was on vacation, but because she was in protective custody. Or the closest unofficial thing to it.

That, however, was something she was determined not to think about—at least not until she left this hotel. Because the truth was, staying here was an exceptional treat, and she intended to enjoy it, and it would be all the better when Mina arrived. Brent had said he was going to send her over to keep Taylor company, and Reece had reminded her of that when he left, ordering her to check the peephole before opening the door.

Now, Taylor was looking forward to putting on a mindless chick flick, ordering a bottle of wine from room service, and spending two luxurious hours just hanging out and not thinking about everything that was screwed up in her life.

She spent the first hour after Reece left reading a romance novel on her phone, then realized her stomach was growling. She glanced at the clock and saw that Mina should be there within the hour, depending on how much time she spent hanging out with Cam and the rest after the contest.

With a sigh, she rolled over and hugged her pillow.

She wanted to be there, too, and she hated that some asshole had made her scared of her own shadow. More than that, though, she couldn't shake the fear that Brent was wrong, and that the brick wasn't unrelated. Maybe her stalker was just making use of the situation.

And if the brick had been about her, then she was putting her friends in danger. The wreck with Jenna could have been so much worse. Hell, just having a crazy stalker put her friends in danger, because who knew when he might go off the rails? He might even grab Mina on the way up, forcing her to use the key that was waiting for her at the front desk to grant access to the floor.

The thought set Taylor's heart to pounding.

No.

Maybe Reggie had gone overboard into the sea of absurd crushes, but surely he hadn't completely snapped.

Had he?

It might not be Reggie…

That thought, however, wasn't even worth considering. Because if she did consider it, it would stick in her head like glue and fear would run like ice water through her veins.

No, it was Reggie. Landon would scare him

shitless, the department would expel him—surely the University had some relevant code of conduct —and he'd slink away back home. Ohio, she thought. Wasn't that where he said his parents lived?

And in the meantime, she was safe in this little Winston Hotel cave, and she was going to damn well enjoy it. Stretching, she grabbed up the phone, punched the button for room service, then ordered a quesadilla, chips and salsa, and a pitcher of margaritas. Screw wine. Tonight was worthy of the hard stuff.

While she waited, she stripped out of the jeans and Tee she'd been wearing all day, then snuggled into the hotel robe. It was soft and fluffy and she breathed deep, enjoying the freshly washed scent with a hint of lavender. She brushed her hair, tried out the moisturizer that was on the bathroom counter, then smelled the shampoo and conditioner. Quality stuff.

Right as she was leaving, there was a sharp tap at the door, and she jumped before remembering that it had to be room service, a conclusion that was confirmed when the deep voice announced, "Room service!" only seconds later. She checked the peephole, saw the guy with the tray, and opened the door.

"Good evening, Ms. D'Angelo," he said. "Where would you like this?"

She turned to point as she said, "On the desk would be great. My friend and I are going to have a movie night." Then she turned back to close the door and had to swallow a scream.

Landon.

Relief flooded through her, and without thinking, she reached out and shoved him back, her palm flat against his chest. "Jerk! You scared me to death."

His hand closed over hers, holding her palm in place. She could feel his body heat through the APD T-shirt he wore, not to mention the tightness of those superior muscles. She felt more than that, too. A sexual charge, a seductive shimmer, a wild awareness. She didn't know what to call it. All she knew was that it had engulfed her, stealing her breath and making her hope beyond all reason that he'd keep holding her hand against his chest forever.

Oh. My. God.

Roughly, she yanked her hand free, breaking the spell, though a few isolated sizzles remained. Her breasts felt tight. And she was suddenly very aware of her inner thighs and parts in-between. Not only that, but she was aware that she was naked under the robe.

For a moment, they just looked at each other, and she thought she might drown in those dark chocolate eyes. Not a bad way to go, really...

Then he took another step toward her, and all the tiny hairs on her body started to vibrate in anticipation of another touch. But he was only stepping aside to let the room service guy pass, his polite, "Have a good evening," lingering in the air after the door closed behind him.

"Land—" she began, but he cut her off with a sharp, "What the *hell* do you think you were doing?"

Her eyes went wide and she took a step back. "Me? What?"

"You're here for your protection, Taylor. But you left the door wide open. You didn't even know I'd stepped in." Those usually kind eyes were hard now, his kissable mouth pulled into a thin, angry line, and she reacted in kind, straightening her spine as she prepared to do battle.

But then she took a closer look. *Not angry*, she realized. *Afraid.*

The tension left her body with an almost audible *whoosh*. "Oh, God. I—I'm sorry."

Immediately, he relaxed as well, then scrubbed his hand over his close-shaved head. "No, I'm sorry. I shouldn't have yelled. But, dammit, I want to trust that you'll be safe even when I'm not there to watch over you."

She turned away, stepping further into the room to hide the smile that danced immediately to her lips. "I guess that means you took the job, despite the low pay and terrible hours."

He chuckled, and when she turned back again, he was right there, having followed her all the way in with amazingly quiet footsteps for such a big man. Taylor was five-eight, pretty tall for a woman, but she still had to look up to see his eyes. Though, honestly, she probably shouldn't. He had the sexiest eyes she'd ever seen. *Bedroom eyes.*

And here they were in a bedroom. How interesting was that?

Stop it.

"What?"

She cringed, realizing she'd spoken aloud. "Just telling myself to stop being stupid. I've taken self-defense courses. And I'm pretty much addicted to romantic suspense novels. I'm really not too stupid to live. You're totally right that I should have shut the door. I was just … in awe, I guess."

"Awe?"

She lifted a shoulder, feeling silly. "This place," she admitted. "I've never stayed any place like it."

He glanced around, obviously taking in the room. The dresser, the desk, the sofa. And, of course, the bed. Maybe it was her imagination, but she thought his eyes lingered on the bed.

"It's nice," he said. "But not that different from most hotels."

"I wouldn't know." She leaned against the edge of the desk. "This is my first hotel."

"Really?"

She only shrugged, not wanting to dig into the details of her rough background.

He was studying her, his head cocked as if she'd surprised him. Considering most people her age had stayed at a hotel—even if it was just a Disney vacation when they were little—his surprise was probably justified.

"Well, you'll have time to enjoy it. I figure two days. We'll get security installed at your apartment, then you can stay there. Tomorrow we'll go grab you some clothes and essentials, and we can talk to your manager."

She nodded, a little numb that things were moving so fast. Fast was good. But it was making her mind spin.

"So how come you're here? Not that I'm ungrateful, but I got the impression from Brent that I'd see you tomorrow. Assuming I saw you at all."

"Was there really any doubt?" He took a step toward her, and she realized that she was trapped between him and the desk. "You honestly thought that I'd say no?"

"I—" Her heart was pounding in her chest. "I guess I wasn't sure. You don't really know me, after all."

The corner of his lip twitched, and his eyes stayed locked on hers. "No? Well, I guess we can remedy that now. And as for helping you, that's what I do, remember?"

"Sure. Right." Her head was spinning. On the one hands, his words suggested he'd come specifically for her. On the other, he was talking as if she was just one more case on his docket.

Instead of pondering that more closely, she deflected. "What about Mina? She's probably on her way over right now."

"I told her I wanted a chance to talk with you first. That you'd text her when we were done."

"Right." Taylor nodded, then cocked her head. "So is this the part where you take my statement, Detective?"

He lifted a brow, his gaze skimming over her. It suddenly struck her that those words sounded more than a little like a come on, and some naughty part deep inside wondered how he'd react if she put her hand back on his chest, and whispered, *Maybe you need to frisk me, too.*

Stop it.

Maybe there was a mutual attraction and maybe there wasn't. But he was in this room to help her, not to take her to bed. And right then she needed help one hell of a lot more than she needed an orgasm.

So get your damn libido under control and stick with the program.

With those strict instructions ringing in her ears, she moved past him to take a seat on the sofa. She started to tuck her foot under her, remembered she was wearing a bathrobe, then pressed both feet to the floor, her legs tight together and her hands resting on her knees.

She cleared her throat. "All right. Interrogation time. What do you want to know?"

"Everything." He perched on the side of the

bed opposite her. "I heard it from Brent. Now I want to hear it from you."

"Right. Of course you do." She'd told Brent. She'd told Reece. Pretty much all she did was talk about how she was in trouble. But she dutifully repeated the whole thing to him. He didn't interrupt, but seemed to take it all in, nodding slowly throughout.

"And now we're here," she said, finally wrapping up.

"Okay. Now tell me more about Reggie."

"Oh." She frowned. She'd repeated the story so many times with so few questions, she hadn't been prepared to go deeper. "Well, I don't know much."

"You said he told you that he'd been working up the courage to ask you out, and you turned him down when he actually managed that."

She lifted her brows. "You're making me sound like a bitch."

"What? For not going out with a guy you weren't interested in? Definitely not a bitch. You did him a kindness. Unless he's a psychopath," he added, amusement flickering in his eyes. "In which case, you just triggered him into stalking you."

She bit back a laugh as she rolled her eyes, immediately feeling better. She hadn't realized how tense she'd been until that tiny bit of laughter loosened her up.

He flashed a mischievous smile, and that time she couldn't help it. She laughed out loud.

"Did he try to ask you out again?"

She shook her head. "Nope. That was it."

"Have you seen him with other girls since?"

She thought back, trying to picture the common area near the entrance to the drama department. "Yeah. I think so. But I'm not sure if he was dating any of them."

"And his full name?"

"Reginald Carter."

Landon tapped something onto his phone, then met her eyes. "We'll talk to him tomorrow, okay? Do you know when he'll be on campus?"

"Sure. Dr. Bishop's class meets tomorrow. I'm not scheduled to help him out, but we can go by."

"Good. That's step one of our plan. I'll see what I can find out about Reggie in the meantime."

A loose thread on her robe caught her attention, and she started to twist it around one finger. "Do we have a step two?"

"There's always a step two. This time it centers on you."

"On me?"

He nodded. "Anyone else come to mind?"

Taylor looked down, saw that the tip of her finger was purple, and sighed. She wanted to stay quiet—because God knew she didn't want to invite those ghosts into her life—but at the same time, she wasn't an idiot.

And the ghosts might already be there.

"There was a guy. Beau. He—well, he had a pretty intense crush on me about eight years ago."

"That's a long time." He leaned back, studying her. "The guy must be dangerous if he's still on your radar. Or if you're still on his."

Her mouth went dry. "Very. He's done time. He's—well, he's not a nice guy. And he wasn't happy when I, um, didn't return his affection. And he knows that I like musicals. I've liked them my whole life. So he could fit with the notes."

"He's here in Austin?"

"No, that's the thing. This was in Arkansas."

"You don't have an accent."

"I worked hard to lose it. Watched a lot of movies and tried to copy the stars' voices." She smiled, sliding into the memory. "I liked the idea of being someone else."

He cocked his head, his expression gentle. "That bad?"

"I—" She licked her lips. She hadn't meant to give so much away. "Yeah. Yeah, it was that bad."

Slowly, he nodded. "Me, too."

Their eyes met, and for a moment, it was just the two of them. No victim. No detective. Just Taylor and Landon and this thing between them that they shared.

She shook herself, forcing the moment to evaporate, then cleared her throat and pushed on. "Being in Austin made it that much easier to lose the accent. Not much of a Texas twang here."

A brief hesitation as he watched her, then he inclined his head, as if acknowledging the change in tone. "And yeehaw to that, little lady."

She laughed, feeling better.

For a moment, he studied her. "Okay, Beau is on the list. What's his full name?"

"Beauregard Clement Harkness."

He double checked the spelling with her, then typed that into his phone. When he looked up at her again, his expression was as serious as she'd ever seen it. "I want you to make me a list of anyone else you think it could be. *Could.* I want comprehensive. You're in theater. You like theater. Anyone who knows you, knows that. Which means anyone might use the theater references."

"Okay." The task was daunting, and not one she wanted to undertake.

"Don't worry about ranking them." He pushed off the bed and stood. "We'll talk about that later."

"You're leaving?" She heard the panic in her voice and wished she'd kept her mouth shut. She stood, then continued, hoping she sounded calmer. "That's all we need to talk about?"

He reached out, his fingers closing on a fold of the robe. There was no physical connection, and yet she felt it. Felt *him*.

"You're safe right now. And I need to get to work. I've got calls to make before we visit Reggie tomorrow."

"Right. Of course. I just—"

He released her robe, but took a single step closer. "Do you want me to stay?"

Yes. Oh, dear God please, yes.

She shook her head, the potency of that thought freaking her out. "No," she blurted. "I have Mina, right? We're going to wallow in a girls' night."

"Just like college girls do."

She lifted a brow. "In case you missed the memo, Mina's out of school. I'm in grad school, and I'll be done at the end of this semester. Then me and my adult ass are hightailing it to LA, where I'm going to make a huge splash in Hollywood. And not as the next Black Dahlia, thank you very much."

"Because I'm going to nail his sorry ass for you."

"Damn right."

He held out his hand, and she took it without thinking, with no time to prepare for that overwhelming sense of connection. That intense craving, like a wild hunger curling inside her.

"Give me your key." His voice sounded husky to her, and she blushed. Not because of the heat in his voice, but because she'd so completely misread the purpose of his extended hand.

"I—why?"

"Nobody but me comes in without a code word. Do you understand? Room Service, friends, nobody."

"A code word?"

"You give it to them when you call. They say it to you when they arrive."

"Oh." She drew a breath, then slowly released it. "You really do think I'm in trouble, don't you?"

He touched her face. "I think I'm not taking any chances with you."

Chapter Five

"HOW?" Mina asked, tossing her head back and moaning dramatically. "How did we finish off an entire pitcher of margaritas?" She flopped back on the bed and sighed. "I'm going to be so ridiculously hung over tomorrow."

"I'll be right there with you," Taylor admitted.

"But it was worth it, right?"

"Oh, yeah," Taylor agreed. They'd gone into the evening intending to watch something silly and fun and girly, like *Bridesmaids* or *Girls Trip*. They'd ended up watching *Magic Mike*, because Mina had said it was like a theme, what with the Man of the Month contest, and since Taylor had missed tonight's contest...

"Are you saying I missed *that* level of strutting?" Taylor had teased.

"Funny. Now pass the remote and the chips."

Now, hours later, they were both paying the price for their evening of debauchery, and as they stretched out on the bed in a margarita haze, Mina sighed, rolled onto her side, and said, "Okay, spill."

"What?" Taylor was pretty sure she knew, but was willing to feign innocence as long as it took.

"Don't give me that. Detective Hottie. Landon. What's the deal?"

"No deal," Taylor said. She opened her eyes, noticed that the ceiling was moving counterclockwise, and shut them again.

"Oh, please. I've known you since high school."

"Only since senior year." Nobody knew her before senior year. She'd been a long way from Austin in more ways than one.

An unexpected shiver cut through her. One person knew her before senior year—*Beau*. But surely he wasn't here.

Please, let him not be here.

Mina continued on, unaware of Taylor's shift in mood. "Senior year or not, the point is, I know you. And I've seen you watching him every time we've seen him at The Fix."

"Why wouldn't I? He's gorgeous."

"Agreed," Mina said. "But so are a lot of the

guys who hang out there, and you don't slap your eagle eye onto them."

"I don't do that!" Did she? The possibility was positively mortifying.

"You do. But there's good news, too." Mina pressed her lips together, looking smug. And obviously staying quiet until Taylor begged.

"Okay. I give up. What's the good news?"

Mina shifted sideways on the bed so that she could shoulder bump Taylor, and when she spoke, it was in a low, secretive whisper. "I've seen him watching you, too."

The statement awakened a flurry of butterflies inside Taylor. "Really?"

She could hear the hope in her voice and wanted to kick herself. Not only for revealing too much to Mina, but also because she was being ridiculous to even think about something with Landon.

Mina nodded, looking pleased with herself.

"Not that it matters," Taylor said, hoping that saying it out loud would drill that reality into her. "Nothing's going to happen."

"It might," Mina chirped as she sat up. "What? That would be a bad thing?" She frowned as she studied Taylor's face, her brow crumpled in confusion. "I mean, it's not like you have to marry the guy. But why not see where it leads?"

"Maybe," Taylor said, wishing that she could. Wondering if it would work. But how could it? Him being a cop, and her being, well, *her.* "I'm just—"

"What?"

Not like other girls.

Too damn attracted to the man.

Scared.

"Not in the mood to talk about it." She snatched the remote and aimed it at the television. "We need more girlfriend time," she said, scrolling to *Girls Trip.* "Okay?"

To Taylor's relief, Mina flopped back against her pillow. "Hell to the yes. And we need another pitcher. Time to really get this party started, right?"

"Absolutely," Taylor said, reaching for the phone. But it was a lie. Because right then, the only way she wanted to party was with Landon. And that simply wasn't going to happen.

LANDON WAS up before dawn hanging the newly painted cabinet doors in his kitchen. A silver-gray that caught and reflected the light from a wall of windows overlooking his tiny East Austin backyard, making the small kitchen seem bigger. The work was harder than it looked, requiring him to balance the heavy solid wood doors as he lined up and reattached the hinges.

But he was grateful for both the physical labor and the concentration needed. He'd barely slept an hour, and dammit, he needed to burn off some excess energy. Plus, he needed something other than fantasies of Taylor filling his head.

Not that he'd spent the whole night fantasizing. He'd got in some work, too. Before he'd tried to catch some sleep, he'd practically burned up the phone, calling in at least a half-dozen favors.

He'd learned that Reggie was as clean as a whistle. Not that his lack of a record exonerated him, but if the guy had psychopathic tendencies, experience had taught Landon that there'd probably be something there, even if it was a sealed juvie record. But there was nothing.

He was still waiting to hear about Beau. He'd tracked down a friend of a friend who had connections in Arkansas. So far, he hadn't heard back, and that was making him antsy.

Taylor had told him about the guy, which was good, but Landon knew damn well she was keeping something back. He assumed they'd had a relationship and that Beau had abused her, and that she either didn't want to admit that she'd been a victim, or he'd scared her so badly that she was truly afraid that talking about what happened would make it worse.

He'd find out, though. And then he'd take great pleasure in making the motherfucker's life a living hell.

By six, every cabinet door had been rehung, and a pleasant ache permeated his arms. By seven, he was showered and changed.

And by eight, he was walking through the front door of The Winston Hotel.

He used the key he'd taken from Taylor last night to access her floor, then reached her room right as the room service guy arrived with a tray topped with a pot of coffee and a bowl of fruit.

"I can take that for you," Landon said, then used his key to open the door. He pushed it open a few inches with his hip, then took the tray, calling, "Taylor? Mina?" before stepping inside.

He got no answer, but heard water running, so he continued inside, calling out, "Hey, I'm here," as he walked past the closed bathroom door to set the tray on the desktop.

Behind him, the bathroom door opened, and he turned, expecting to find Taylor stepping out to say hi.

Instead he saw Taylor. *All* of Taylor. She was looking down as she rubbed a towel over her damp hair, and every luscious inch of her was entirely naked.

Landon's brain knew that he should make a sound. A noise. Anything to let her know that he was there. But the rest of him wasn't cooperating. His mouth had gone dry. His cock was rock hard. His fingers twitched with an almost palpable need to touch those luscious curves. And his eyes...

Oh, dear Lord, his eyes were looking at heaven. That rich, tanned skin that would feel so smooth beneath his fingers. Those sleek, muscled thighs that could wrap so tight around him as he fucked her senseless. Her perfect round breasts, her nipples tight and teasing, as if begging him to suck hard before falling to his knees, closing his mouth over that glorious, waxed pussy, and feasting on the taste of her.

He made a rough, raw noise in his throat, and her head snapped up, her eyes wide as he stupidly thrust out his hand, as if blocking her from sight. In one swift motion, she yanked the towel down, turned on her heel, and barreled into the bathroom.

"I'm sorry!" he called. "Shit, Taylor, I thought you heard me come in."

"What the hell! Oh, my God, what the hell?"

"I know, I know, I'm sorry. I didn't mean— *Shit.*"

A moment later the door opened again and she slipped out, once again wearing that fluffy hotel bathrobe. Her face was bright red, and as he imagined the blush creeping down, he was suddenly overwhelmed with the urge to strip off that damn robe, then follow the line of red down her bare skin with his tongue.

Down, boy.

She cleared her throat, then sat primly on the foot of the bed. "Did you find anything about Reggie?

"Not much." He told her what he'd learned, and she nodded.

"So that means it's probably not him?"

"Not necessarily." He sat on the bed next to her, then shifted a bit so that he could look at her more directly. As he did, his knee brushed hers. He saw her stiffen, but she didn't move away.

"Why not necessarily?"

"Every criminal has a first time," he said. "You might be his."

A wry smile played at her mouth. "Yay for me."

"When was the first note?" he asked. "Did anything happen right before? With Reggie, I mean."

"Like a trigger?"

He nodded, then watched her face as she concentrated, noting the adorable vertical crease above her nose. Christ, but she was lovely. All of her unique features pulling together to create an image that drew him in and painted a picture on his heart.

Inwardly, he winced. He had it bad if she was inspiring him to think such flowery, sappy thoughts. Inconvenient as hell, but apparently his attraction to Taylor was his new reality.

She started to shake her head, but he caught her chin with the tip of his finger. "Go deeper," he said. "Had you gotten a position in a show that he wanted? Had you cut him off at the soda machine? Did he see you talking with another man?"

Her mouth opened, those soft lips parting as if readying for a kiss. "Yes," she said, and for one crazed moment, he thought she was inviting his lips to hers. Then he realized she was answering his question.

"Another man? Where? Who?"

"I—I bumped into him. At the Broken Spoke," she said, referencing an iconic Austin dance hall. "A group of us had gone out after one of the Man of the Month contests. We do that sometimes, but this time Brent was with us."

"Unusual for him because of Faith," Landon said, and Taylor nodded.

"He was teaching me how to two-step. I saw Reggie across the bar watching us."

"When was that?"

She thought back. "After Parker. So, about two weeks ago. And about a week before the brick."

"Hang on." He tapped out a quick text to Brent, asking if he remembered the night, and if he'd noticed anyone watching him afterwards, or if anything odd had happened to him or his car. The answer was immediate and negative. Brent hadn't noticed a thing.

Considering Brent's training—and his tendency to be extra observant about his home because of Faith—Landon had to assume there'd been no incidents aimed at him. But that didn't mean the perp wasn't Reggie. His focus might be narrowed to the woman he coveted, punishing her for her perceived infidelity.

Assuming it was Reggie at all.

"There's something else," Taylor said. "That's about the time I started to feel—"

"What?"

"Watched, I guess. I didn't mention it before because it's just a feeling." She licked her lips, clearly pondering something.

"There's something else?"

"It's just ... I know you said anyone could quote musicals to me, but that just seems so much more of a Reggie thing. And Beau was eight years and a lot of miles ago. Plus—"

He cocked his head. "Plus what?"

But she only shook her head. "Plus it seems so unlikely after all this time that he'd find me. That he'd even try. Doesn't it?"

Before Landon could answer, she plowed on, as if determined to convince herself that Beau couldn't have a thing to do with this. "And he's not exactly cultured. Or he wasn't. I mean, he knows I like musicals, but I'm not sure he'd do a good job picking the quotes. I mean, he was the kind of guy who cleans under his toenails with a switchblade. He probably thinks *Evita* is a soda pop and *Sweeney Todd* the name of a pirate in those Johnny Depp movies. Quotes from *Grease* would be more likely."

"I haven't gotten any intel back on him. Not yet. And we haven't seen him in Austin. But he's the one you're scared of."

"Of course I'm scared of him. He's a scary guy." She stood up and went to the desk, then started to pour herself a cup of coffee.

"What aren't you telling me, Taylor?"

Her back was too him, but as she picked up the cup, he saw that her hands were shaking. "Nothing."

She turned, then looked straight at him, long lashes surrounding wide, guileless brown eyes. "Absolutely nothing," she repeated.

And he knew without a doubt that she was lying.

Chapter Six

IN ALL HER years at the University of Texas, Taylor had never been inside Memorial Stadium, the shrine to football that dominated the east side of campus, near the LBJ Library and the Texas Performing Arts Center. But because she'd pretty much lived her entire college life in the PAC, she'd seen the stadium every single day.

Now, they were walking down the hill toward the drama department, the stadium looming to their left, and Landon's car parked illegally behind them, an APD placard on the dashboard to keep it from getting ticketed.

"Cheater," she teased as they walked side by side, but he only grinned at her like a boy in a candy store. "The job's got perks. Gotta enjoy them."

"Perks," she said. "Interesting…" She let her voice trail off, not quite believing that she was being so bold. But ever since she'd stood naked in front of him she hadn't been able to get the expression on his face out of her mind. She'd seen hard, animal lust more than once in her life, but that wasn't what had colored Landon's face.

No, she'd seen desire. Longing. A potent, ripe need. Hell, she'd seen appreciation. And every flicker on his face, every spark in his eyes had been like looking in a mirror.

He wanted her, too. And though she knew she should back away slowly, the truth was, she didn't want to. Or maybe she did. She wasn't sure. And that uncertainty was driving her boldness. Because if she pushed and he answered in kind…

Well, then the decision would be made for her.

Not the permanent kind, God forbid. But maybe it would be okay to let herself go with this man, at least for a little bit.

She cast a sideways glance at him, remembering how it had felt. Not just her reaction to his expression, but the act of being naked in front of him. Yeah, she'd bolted and cried out, but that was more out of surprise than any sort of negative feelings.

On the contrary, once the shock had worn off,

desire had fired her skin. She'd pressed her back to the bathroom door and breathed, fantasizing about what would have happened if she'd simply walked toward him, inviting him to touch her.

She hadn't had the courage, though. But now … well, maybe now she wanted to poke at that question and see where their attraction led … and to hope that it led to bed, and to Landon between her thighs.

"Was that one of them?" she asked, spitting the words out quickly before she changed her mind.

He paused on the sidewalk, his face a question mark.

"Seeing me naked. Was that a job perk?"

His Adam's apple rose and fell, and for a moment she thought he wasn't going to answer. Then he looked boldly into her eyes. "Damn right it was."

They stood like that for a moment, simply looking at each other. Then a skateboarder zipped past, and she jumped, and that was it. The spell was broken.

"Come on," he said. "That class will be letting out soon."

"Right." She fell in step beside him, cursing whatever idiotic policy let skateboarders on sidewalks—was that even allowed? But then Landon reached for her hand. She looked up, surprised, and saw his cocky grin.

"We're trying to bait him, remember. What better way than to look like a couple, right?"

She nodded, her throat feeling strangely thick.

A few more steps and they reached the intersection. They were catty-corner to the drama building, and crossed diagonally when it was clear, then entered the building. A common area was just off the main hall, with tables, chairs, and some tattered sofas. Landon led them to a sofa, and even when they were seated, he kept a tight hold on her hand.

"Did you go to UT?" she asked, when the silence became too much for her.

He shook his head. "No. I grew up in Austin, but I went to St. Edwards," he told her, naming a private college located south of the river. "Got my bachelor's in criminal justice, then joined the Marines."

"Really? How long did you serve?"

"Four years. I went in as an officer, but never intended it to be a career. But my father—well, my foster father—served and I wanted to as well."

"But you wanted to be a cop."

"I wanted to be a detective," he clarified.

"And you are. That's great."

"I like to think so." He lifted their joined hands and lightly kissed the base of her thumb. Her eyes widened with surprise, but he nodded toward the hall where students were starting to emerge. "Want to play it right. Make him jealous. And who wouldn't be jealous of a beautiful girl with me, even if I am old enough to be off your radar?"

She didn't disagree, even if he was being silly. But as he pulled her to her feet and they started scanning the faces, she asked him how old he was.

"Thirty-six. And you're what? Twenty-four?"

"Almost twenty-five."

"Hmm," he said, and she tightened her grip on his hand, certain that naming the gap between them was going to make him tug free. And they needed to look like a couple. For the act they were putting on for Reggie, she told herself. She was just thinking about their investigation, and he was the one who suggested the whole dating pretense.

"You think this is a jealousy thing?" Her thoughts brought the question to the forefront.

"I think it's damn likely."

"But what will we—oh, there he is." She lifted a hand, catching Reggie's attention. He smiled, didn't seem at all distressed to see her, and hurried over, a lanky colt of a guy.

"Hey, Taylor!" His eyes cut to Landon. "Sorry, if we've met. I don't remember you."

"Landon," he released Taylor's hand and shook Reggie's. "I'm not a student."

Reggie nodded, but didn't seem fazed. His attention shifted back to Taylor. "Were you supposed to be in class today?"

"No, we're just here because, well…" She looked helplessly up at Landon, not sure how this was supposed to work exactly.

"To be honest, someone's been bothering Taylor." Landon's eyes were locked on Reggie. So were hers for that matter. As far as she could tell, his reaction was entirely normal—concern mixed with confusion.

"Bothering?"

"You know her pretty well," Landon continued, ignoring Reggie's question. "Anyone else you can think of who knows she likes Sondheim? Or even just musical theater?"

"Sondheim?" He blinked, then frowned. "I don't know. I mean, I think you mentioned it once or twice in class, didn't you?"

She nodded. She'd forgotten about that, but she'd talked at length about *Into The Woods* one class.

"Have you noticed anyone watching her?" Landon's questions were rapid fire, and Taylor assumed that was to prevent Reggie from having a chance to think.

"What's going on?" Reggie demanded, looking between the two of them.

"She's received some nasty notes," Landon said, taking a single step toward Reggie. Not threatening, but definitely edging into his personal space. "And I intend to stop whoever's sending them."

"Shit, yeah." He looked over Landon's shoulder to Taylor. "You okay?"

She nodded.

"So, how else can I help?"

Landon took a step back, then once again twined his fingers with Taylor's. "If you think of anything else—or if anyone asks about her—let Taylor know. Or, hell, call me." He fished a business card out of his pocket and handed it over.

Reggie glanced down, then back up again. "You're a cop?"

"That's right. But this isn't an official investigation." He released her hand and put an arm around her, and without thinking she leaned against him, safe in his embrace. "I'm just protecting my girl."

Reggie nodded. "Good. Shit, Taylor, this is wild. I'll let you know, okay?"

"Thanks, Reggie," she said, then watched as he hitched his backpack higher on his shoulder then headed toward the main exit. He was about to push through the doors when he turned back. "Hey, what about that reporter?"

Taylor and Landon exchanged a glance, then hurried toward Reggie.

"What reporter?" Taylor asked.

"This dude from the *Daily Texan,*" he said, referring to the student newspaper. "An older guy. Said he was a grad student in the journalism department, and that he was doing a profile piece on you."

She looked up at Landon, then gave a small shake of her head. She didn't know a thing about anything like that.

"Does this guy have a name?"

"Yeah, but I'm not sure I can—oh, wait. Buddy. I remember because that was the name of my first dog. And his last name was—give me a sec. Oh, right. Hall. His last name was Hall. I remember because I used to live in Carothers Hall before I moved off campus."

Taylor said nothing, but she tightened her grip on Landon's hand and willed her legs not to turn to rubber.

"Do you think that had something to do with all this note stuff?" Reggie asked.

"Oh, I doubt it." She forced her voice to stay light, but the way Landon was looking at her, she had a feeling she wasn't succeeding. "I'm pretty sure he's the guy who left a voicemail for me about an article. That must have been what it was about. But let me know if he talks to you again." She forced a smile. "If I'm gonna be famous, it would be nice to know what's going to be said about me."

"True that. And will do."

They said goodbye again, and as soon as Reggie disappeared through the doors, Taylor sagged against the wall, Landon right beside her.

"Tell me," he said, and she nodded.

"I—yes. Just give me a minute, okay? I wasn't— I just wasn't expecting that."

He studied her, those dark eyes seeming to see all the way into her soul. Then he nodded, and took her hand. "It's turning into a beautiful day. There's someplace I want to show you."

She allowed him to lead her outside, then back the way they came. They headed up the street in front of the stadium, and he surprised her by turning inside.

"Fortification," he said, leading her to a Starbucks. "Coffee and conversation."

"We're hanging out inside the stadium?"

"Trust me," he said, then led her back outside once they had their coffees in hand. They continued in the same direction until they reached the fountain and the grass-covered hills at the base of the LBJ Presidential Library.

He took her hand and led her up almost to the copse of trees, then sat on the grass—tugging her down beside him.

They sat that way for a while, looking at the round fountain below, the Texas History Center to the right, the presidential library in front of them, and the stadium and the full expanse of the University campus off to their left.

"When I was a kid, I used to come here in the summer, pretend like it was snowing, and ride a piece of cardboard down this hill," he said. "It was my attempt at having a normal life."

"How old?"

"About seven. Maybe eight."

"Your parents brought you?"

He shook his head. "I'd ride my bike."

Her eyes widened in surprise. "Your parents let you do that?"

His laugh was more of a scoff. "My dad would shove me out of the house in the mornings, tell my mother I needed to go out into the world and be a man, and that I could come back for dinner."

Since she wasn't sure what to say, she didn't say anything at all.

"He disappeared right before I turned nine. We think it was a gang killing—that was the kind of neighborhood I lived in—but I've never known for sure."

"So you were raised with a single mom?"

"Only for about a year. And during that year, the gang life was tugging at me. I mean, really tugging. They knew I'd lost my dad and were ramping up, trying to suck me in."

"What did you do?" She tried to picture him, the honorable man she knew him to be as a child trying to find his way.

"I dodged. I kept my nose clean. I spent more time fighting to keep out of that life than I did trying to figure out my schoolwork. And all the time I kept wishing that I'd find an escape. A way out.

Away from the death and the drugs and the bullshit."

"It never happened?" She heard the pain in his voice and assumed that was where the story was going.

"Oh, I got free." His words were sharp with regret. "Be careful what you wish for, right?"

She pressed her lips together, afraid of what was coming.

"A drive-by. One minute my mother was laughing in our front yard. The next she was dead. I was nine. The next thing I knew, I was in foster care."

She reached out and took his hand, hoping that somehow she could draw off some of the pain she heard in his voice.

"I got what I wished for, but talk about a price."

"I'm so sorry."

"She was a good woman. My rock when I was trying to stay clean. She didn't deserve to die. She wasn't even thirty."

Taylor blinked, and an errant tear trickled down the side of her nose. "Your childhood doesn't sound easy." Hers had been hard, too. She understood the hell of growing up like that, scared and feeling alone. "What happened?"

A smile touched his lips. "It got better. Hell, it's still getting better."

"You landed in a good family?"

"The best. I consider them my parents, and vice-versa, although they never formally adopted me. I—well, I felt it would be an insult to my mom."

"I get that."

"But they gave me a home. An education. A safe neighborhood where the kids think the kind of childhood I had only happens on television, not a few miles away on the other side of the highway. At any rate, things have been getting better. A few bumps along the way, but for the most part, life is looking up." He smiled at her, the kind of smile that warmed her from the inside. "Of course, I've had help. My foster parents. My commanding officer. My partner."

"You have a partner?"

He nodded. "Well, I did. He just retired and moved to New Mexico. That's part of why I took vacation now. Figured I'd take a break before they assign me a new one."

"Thanks for telling me all of that."

"You're welcome." He leaned toward her, then

spoke in a conspiratorial whisper. "But you're missing the subtext."

"Am I?"

"You're supposed to share, too."

"I…"

"I saw the look on your face. Buddy Hall. Beauregard Harkness. You think it's the same guy."

"No," she said, her voice barely more than a whisper. "I don't *think* it is. I'm certain of it."

Chapter Seven

"HE HAD this obsession with Buddy Holly," Taylor told him once they were back in his car. "Holly. Hall. Get it?"

"I get it." Landon had already started the car and shifted into reverse, but now he turned to her, his gaze hard enough to make her squirm. "I get that there's no question left. This guy from Arkansas tracked you to Austin. This guy from eight years ago followed you here and is gaslighting you. We both know it. Don't we?"

Slowly, she nodded.

"What I don't know is why. But I think you do."

"He's fucked up," she said, and wasn't that the damn truth? Never in her life had she brushed up against anyone as messed up as Beauregard Harkness.

Landon's hands tightened on the steering wheel. His eyes closed, and she was absolutely certain that he was counting to ten. Finally, he drew a breath and looked at her again. As calm as a pond on a still winter morning. "I want to help you, Taylor. Hell, I think it would probably kill me to fail you. To watch you get hurt. But I can't do it alone. You have to help me. You have to tell me everything."

Fear-soaked cotton seemed to fill her throat, blocking the words that wanted to burst out. She wanted to tell him everything—the whole sordid, horrible tale. But it wouldn't come. Instead, she just shook her head. She couldn't do it. Couldn't stand the thought that he'd see another version of her.

A Taylor who wasn't a Taylor at all.

She closed her eyes, counted to ten, and then slowly shook her head. "I've told you," she finally whispered. "He's bad. No," she corrected. "He's evil. And if he finds me, I swear to God, he'll kill me."

He slammed the gearshift back into Park and turned to her. "Dammit, Taylor, you need to trust me."

"I do." Hot tears streamed down her cheeks, fueled by fear and anger and frustration. She wanted to tell him—she did. But he didn't truly need to know any of it, and telling him would just open doors that were better off closed.

She sucked in a long breath. "But if you really want to help me, then please, just help me stop him. He's bad, Landon. That's the long and the short of it. There's nothing else you need to know."

"Isn't there?"

She shook her head.

"So there's no reason to get to know you?" He reached for her, then pressed his hand against her thigh. She closed her eyes as the warmth from his touch seeped through her. "Don't you get it, Taylor? I don't just want to help you. I want—"

"What?" Her word was barely a whisper.

A beat, then, "I want to know you."

She lifted her chin until she was looking straight at him. "Then we want the same thing. Because you do know me. That girl from before? The girl who left Arkansas? That girl isn't me, Landon. Even I don't know her anymore."

Now, his kind eyes looked sad. But it was true. It was all true.

Bottom line, if he wanted to help her, all he had to do was stop Beau. The rest was just noise.

For a moment, he just looked at her, and she sat stiff in anticipation of his words. Fortunately, the sharp ring of his phone broke the moment. He answered it, glanced at her, then said, "Glad to hear it. Thanks."

When he hung up, she cocked her head. "What?"

"Your security system. It's installed and ready to go."

"That's great. So I can stay at my apartment tonight?"

"Looks that way."

She exhaled in relief. "Not that it wasn't a fun experience, but I prefer being in my own space. Can you take me to the hotel? I left a few things in the bathroom that Mina brought. Plus, I should probably check out, then get my car. I left it in a lot near The Fix."

"I'll take you," he said. "But I want to go through your apartment first. No sense checking out of the hotel if everything's not copacetic."

Since she couldn't argue with that, she nodded, then leaned back as he navigated to her West Campus apartment. A small building, it had five units and was on a narrow lot between two larger complexes.

He pulled into the slot near her unit. Once he killed the engine, she started to open her door, then paused. "You don't have to go in, you know. I can go over everything with Martin," she added, referring to her manager.

His brows rose, but he said nothing.

"I just mean, you know. You've done so much already." That wasn't it, though. That wasn't even close to it. Just the opposite, really. Because it wasn't how much he'd done, but how comfortable she'd become around him. And how much he was pushing. Because what if he pushed harder? And what if she caved?

She could almost see that terrifying future unfolding. Her telling him all those secrets she'd kept locked up for years. Truths that could land her in so much trouble she'd never manage to claw her way out again.

Truths that could get her killed.

Except Landon already knew *that* piece of the truth, because it was Beau who'd be doing the killing.

Anyway you sliced it, the problem was the same —she'd let Landon get too close. And even though a very big part of her wanted him even closer, it was safer to push him away.

Silence hung thick in the air between them, crowding the already cramped interior of the car.

"You're suggesting I just drop you and leave?"

"You've already given up a lot of your time. I'm supposed to be a side project, right? And Martin knows the system. He must since he supervised the install."

"Uh-huh." He opened the door, then started to slide out of the car. "Come on. We're going."

"Landon," she began, but he was already out. She frowned, scooted out, too, then circled the car and met him. "Dammit, I—"

"No." He held up a finger, silencing her. "You either let me check out the apartment, or you come sleep at my house. Your choice. But you're not going in there without me beside you. And for the record, Martin doesn't know the system as well as I do. I ordered it. I arranged it with the installation team. I gave them the initial settings. You want to understand all the bells and whistles? How to stay safe? I'm the guy you need."

"Okay, but—"

"No buts. You say you're supposed to be a side project? Like that's all you are to me? Then fine. Have it your way." She could hear the frustration—maybe even anger—in his voice. "But I'm doing this because Brent asked. And I'm not taking risks with you. He'd have my ass if something happened to you."

"Brent's not the boss of me." Taylor pushed back her hair, trying to sound calm. "Is that the only reason you've been helping me? Because Brent asked you to?"

He made an exasperated noise. "You're an idiot if you think that." His soft tone, as gentle as a caress, washed over her.

He took a single step closer, then spoke even more softly. As if she was a frightened kitten, and he was afraid of startling her. "I don't know what spooked you between our break outside the library and the walk back to the car. Maybe you remembered something. Maybe you saw something. Maybe you're just rolling around too much in your own head. But the bottom line is that I'm watching over you. That's it. The end. So deal the fuck with it, okay?"

She rocked back on her heels, so surprised by such strong words in that soft tone that she couldn't help but laugh. "Okay," she said, out of reflex as much as acquiescence.

"Good. Then let's go in." He put his hand on her shoulder as she inserted her key, and she stiffened, hyperaware of the contact between them, and the way his touch lit a fire inside her.

"Wait here," he said once they'd stepped inside, closed the door behind them, and he'd punched in the code to disarm the alarm. Then he pulled a small gun from his pocket—she hadn't even realized he had it—and proceeded slowly through the place. She watched him move through the living room and kitchen, then heard him opening the closet doors in her bedroom and bathroom.

Finally, he called to her. "Taylor?"

"I'm here. I'm good. But can you—*ah!*" She leaped backward, surprised by a flying brown blob.

Landon was back by her side in an instant, his gun drawn and ready. "What?"

"I—I don't know."

"Maybe you imagined it?"

She wanted to argue, but then she saw the movement again, and she leapt into his arms, clinging tight. Her chest was pressed to those rock-hard abs as his free strong arm curved around her. She felt his position change as he slipped the gun back into the holster that she now saw clipped to the inside of his jeans. And she heard his soft, reassuring voice telling her it was only a cat. *Mr. Patches,* some part of her mind realized. A stray that tended to wander into her place.

Landon still spoke soothing words, but she barely heard them. Instead, all she could hear was the beat of her own blood pounding in her ears. All she could feel was the heat of him pressed hard against her.

She lifted her head, then leaned back enough so that she could look up into his eyes. "Landon," was all she said.

It was enough.

And with one wild, claiming motion, he drew her even tighter against him, so close that she could feel his rock-hard erection pressing against her through his jeans.

At the same time, she heard his low, almost desperate groan. And then, before she even had time to think, his mouth closed hard and hot over hers, taking her in a violent, wonderful, maddening kiss that stripped away all of her defenses, and left only one demanding word in her mind:

More.

Chapter Eight

LANDON WASN'T THINKING as he crushed his mouth against hers, pulling her tight against him. Her shriek had cut through him like a hot blade, and in the split second before he'd reached her, cold terror had cut through him. The fear that he'd lost her when he'd only just found her, and all he'd have left was a hole in his heart.

Roughly, he pulled her tighter against him until he could feel her breasts hard against her chest. One hand cupped the back of her head, and the other slid down, holding her in place with a flat palm at her lower back. She felt like heaven in his arms, but it was the taste of her that drove him wild, not to mention her own enthusiastic response to his kiss.

"Do you have any idea how long I've wanted to

taste you?" he asked, his lips brushing her skin as he spoke.

"Me, too," she murmured, the truth in those words cutting into him, making him even harder than he could imagine.

"I want to feel you. I want to see you again—you're a work of art, baby. Will you strip for me?"

He watched her swallow. Saw her teeth play across her lower lip. He could hear the quiver in her breath before she spoke. "I've never done anything like that."

"Good," he said. "Do it only for me."

"Oh." The word was little more than an exhale, and as he watched, a slow blush rose on her cheeks. But she did as he asked. She moved slowly, not intentionally teasing, but the mere act of watching her undress—of baring herself to her bra and panties simply because he asked her to—well, that was a tease and a turn-on combined, and it made him feel powerful.

More, the fact that she'd obeyed—the trust that revealed—made him feel humble.

And looking at her like that, her smooth skin tinged with the faintest blush, made him harder than he could ever remember being.

"More?"

He nodded, almost too numb to form words. As he did, he noticed that her eyes had dipped to his crotch, and he realized that he was stroking himself through his jeans.

Swallowing, he met her eyes, and almost came right then when he saw her lick her lips, as if silently telling him exactly what she could do with that tongue.

"Take it out," she said. "I want to see you stroke your cock."

He tilted his head. "I don't think so."

"No?" Slowly, her hand dipped inside her panties, and he saw a tremor cut through her as she fingered herself. "Then I guess you don't get to see what's behind the curtain either."

Fuck. He unzipped, freed his cock. And oh, holy hell, he was so damn close.

She looked a little surprised that he'd complied, but she played the game and slowly slid her panties down then unfastened her bra. His cock jumped in his hand as he watched her stroke her own breasts, then tease her nipples to hard nubs.

And when she walked toward him—slowly, like a runway model—it took every ounce of his willpower not to come right then. "Kiss me," she begged. "Please, kiss me."

He pulled her naked body against him, his mouth closing over hers, claiming her with such wild ferocity their teeth clashed as their bodies rubbed together. His cock was so hard he thought he would come right then, and the feel of his erection rubbing against her bare skin right above her pussy had to be one of the most erotic sensations of his life.

"Sit." The word was barely a breath, and he only understood her because she'd pushed him backward toward the couch.

He did as she asked, and she straddled him. He was still fully clothed except for his unzipped jeans and freed cock, and now she straddled it, rubbing her wet pussy over his hard length as if she was determined to make him completely lose his mind.

It was working.

He closed his hands over her breasts, then pinched her nipples, making her cry out. Making her pussy clench so that the intimate movements teased his tumescence, taking him that much closer to exploding.

"Please," she begged, her own hand slipping down to tease her clit—something that was so fucking hot he thought he'd lose it right then. "Please tell me you have a condom."

He did. He had two in his wallet, and he reached back and pulled the wallet free, then managed to find one, all the while making a mental note to buy a jumbo-size box the next time he was at the grocery store.

"Put it on," she said.

"I'm still dressed."

"I know. I like this. I didn't think I would, but I do."

He tilted his head. "What?"

"It being uneven. You seeing me, but me not seeing you. Being naked for you. Open for you." For a moment, uncertainty flashed on her face. "You do like it?"

"Dear God, yes. But Taylor…" He almost forced himself to shut up. To let this keep going and talk later. But he had to be smart with her. With Taylor, he didn't want to screw anything up, and he was too goddamn old for her. And he sure wasn't looking for a relationship. But he wanted her. Oh, damn, how he wanted her.

She shook her head, then pressed a finger to his lips. "Whatever you're going to say, don't. We both want this. And right now, I don't care about tomorrow. Tonight, all I want is you."

SHE MEANT every word she said. She wanted *him*. Landon. She wanted his hands on her, his cock inside her. She wanted his kisses and his soft words.

Right then, she craved him like a drug, and when she held the velvet steel of his cock and positioned the head at her core—when she lowered herself onto him and felt him fill her—well, that's when she knew that she'd discovered what heaven felt like.

Honestly, it felt like Landon.

He did things to her. Incredible things.

Empowering things.

God knew she'd been bolder with him than any other man she'd ever been with, and it had felt incredible to strip for him. To order him to touch himself. To ride him now when he was fully clothed.

"You make me wild," she said.

"Baby, it's mutual. And you make me too damn hot. I need you to ride me hard. I'm so close. So damn close. Come with me."

"Touch me. Take me with you."

His groan was low and passion-filled, and he did as she asked, his fingers finder her clit and stroking her as she clutched his shoulders and rode him hard, impaling him so deep inside her that with each thrust she was teasing her G-spot as he teased her clit, and the sensations swirled through her, building and growing until she couldn't take it anymore.

The prickles of electricity started in the thighs, then seemed to converge on her sex, faster and hotter, until she exploded, her core convulsing, milking him, taking him over with her, his low groan of release so incredibly hot that the sound of his passion alone almost made her come all over again.

When they were both spent, they spooned together on the sofa, his chest to her back so his lips brushed her shoulder and one hand gently teased her sex. "Careful, or you'll find yourself naked this time, and in my bed."

"I can live with that," he said, then sat up. He pulled her up, too, then kissed her. "Where's your phone?"

"Oooh, what sexy pillow talk."

He lifted a brow, and she hurried to pass him her phone from the coffee table.

He pulled out his, too, then fiddled a bit.

"What are you doing?"

"A present," he said, then passed it back, a

tracking app now open on the screen. "Now we can find each other."

"Yeah?" She smiled, warmed that he'd thought of something so simple. "But in case you were wondering, I don't want to have to go looking. I want you to stay right at my side."

He held her eyes for a full beat, and she started to worry that she'd said too much. Then he smiled, slow and sexy. "Baby," he said, "that's exactly what I want, too."

Chapter Nine

TAYLOR WOKE IN HEAVEN. Or, more accurately, to the smell of coffee brewing and bacon frying. Which, as far as she was concerned, was the same thing.

She slipped on a robe, then padded into her kitchen to find Landon poking at a huge skillet of bacon with rubber tongs.

"This is a lovely domestic sight," she said, coming behind him and wrapping her arms around his waist.

He turned around to face her, his eyes roaming over her as a slow smile touched his lips. "Good morning, beautiful. I could get used to this."

"Me, too," she admitted, her body flushing under the intensity of his gaze. The words were scary, but true. This man had shifted things inside her somehow. As if there'd been a chemical reaction between them, and everything she'd been—and feared—had changed its pattern in the night. Now it felt like she had a path through the darkness with Landon beside her. Scary and tentative, but nice. A small blossom forcing its way up through a crack in the concrete.

He brushed his thumb over her lower lip. "Kiss for your thoughts?"

"That's pretty much what I was thinking about," she admitted, then tilted her face up for a slow, deep kiss.

When they broke apart, she was grinning. "Cheater," she said. "You've been picking at the bacon."

"I have," he admitted, then reached for a piece and fed it to her. He kissed her quick afterwards, then pulled back with a twinkle in his eyes. "Delicious."

"Right back at you."

He turned back to the stove to flip the bacon and stir a skillet of scrambled eggs. "I have calls in about Beau," he said. "I should hear back this morning. In the meantime, I thought we could—"

"Wait," she said, putting her hand on his back. "I have a request."

He flipped the heat off under the skillets, then turned to face her.

"I just want—I mean, could we—oh, hell. Can we just pretend like none of this is happening? At least until after you hear back. I want to … well, the truth is I just want to hang out with you. Eat that breakfast you made, cuddle on the couch, maybe read. Watch TV. And then later we could go to The Fix and get my car. You know, normal stuff. Could we? I mean, you know, if you were planning on staying with me, and…"

She trailed off, fearing that she'd presumed too much. But when she saw the slow grin that was lighting those amazing eyes, she knew what his answer would be, and her own smile bloomed wide when he said, "Sweetheart, I think that sounds just about perfect."

Because they'd slept so late, it was past ten when they ended up on the couch with their breakfast plates on the coffee table in front of them. And because he'd been sitting on the doormat when Landon went outside to grab the morning paper, Mr. Patches sat between them, eating the bits of bacon that both Landon and Taylor were sneaking to him.

Afterwards, Taylor curled up with a classic Julie

Garwood novel, and Landon kicked back for a marathon re-watch of the first season of *Game of Thrones*. When she got up to refill her coffee, she came back with two Mimosas and winked at him. It was Friday, but it felt like a luxurious lazy weekend morning. More than that, it felt normal.

No, with Landon beside her, it felt special.

I could get used to this, he'd said. And yeah, so could she.

Despite their laziness, the day seemed to fly by, and when Landon's phone rang, she realized it was already almost five.

He took it, and he mouthed the word *Beau,* so she knew it was from one of his contacts, but she couldn't figure out the gist of the conversation from his monosyllabic side of the conversation.

"Well?" she asked he hung up.

"Pay dirt. Your Mr. Harkness is swimming in warrants. We get our hands on him, not only can we ship him back to Arkansas, but we can pretty much ensure that he spends a very long time behind bars."

Relief flooded her body. "That's so fabulous."

He nodded slowly, as if considering that assessment. "It is," he said, then moved off the couch to sit on the coffee table in front of her. "But it would be a hell of a lot better if you filed a complaint. If this were an official investigation. I could get a team assigned. I could make things happen."

Ice replaced the relief, and she shook her head, then put down the Mimosa she'd been about to sip so he wouldn't notice the way her hand had started shaking. "No," she whispered. "I'm sorry, but no."

She watched the emotions play over his face. Confusion. Frustration. Determination. "I need you to talk to me, Taylor. I need you to tell me what else is going on."

But she just shook her head, then stood. "Please," she said. "No cops. Just you. If you care at all about me, then please just trust me."

He looked like he was going to argue, but instead he nodded. "This conversation isn't over."

"I know." But it was over for now, and she'd take what she could get. "Want to go to The Fix? I'd like to get my car out of that lot. Plus, we can grab a bite."

"Sure."

And just like that the day turned normal again. They were a couple going out for a meal. She half-expected him to tell her not to say anything about the two of them if they bumped into friends in the bar, which, of course, would happen. But he didn't say a word. On the contrary, he took her hand as they walked from the street spot he'd snagged to the glass and wood door of The Fix. And he pressed his palm to her lower back as they entered together.

Once inside, they found a two-top by the window, and they ordered Lobster Rolls. As they waited for their food, Landon went to the back to talk to Brent. As soon as he disappeared, Mina plopped into his chair, and Megan dragged a chair over.

"Well?" Mina asked.

"Why aren't you at work?" Taylor countered.

She waved off the question. "I left right at five. I'm meeting a local director here for dinner. That's not the point. What happened with you and Landon?"

"Wait," Megan said. "What happened that you're staying at The Winston?"

Taylor blinked at her. "How'd you hear about that?"

Megan rolled her eyes. "Small world, or hadn't you noticed? I was at The Winston for a meeting with the conference manager. The Fix is sponsoring a food fair in October and Derek arranged for the hotel to donate space," she added in response to

Taylor's questioning look. "Amanda was there, and we started talking and…"

"Gossip central," Taylor said. "Yeah, I get it. Long story, but the bottom line is that this guy who used to be into me before I moved to Texas is stalking me."

"Shit," Megan said.

"That about sums it up for me," Taylor admitted.

"And Landon's her knight in sexy armor," Mina chirped. "And…?"

Taylor smiled and hummed, then lifted her brow, and both girls squealed.

"So have you … you know?" Mina asked.

"A girl never *you knows* and tells," Taylor quipped, making them both laugh and lean in for more gossip.

Fortunately, Taylor was saved by the arrival of both food and Landon.

"What did I miss?" he asked, which caused Mina and Megan to exchange glances and start giggling all over again.

He shifted his attention to Taylor and lifted a single brow. She just batted her eyes and blew him a kiss.

They hung out for a while after they ate, just

chatting with everyone they knew. Then they headed to the lot to get her car. She wanted to ask Landon what the sleeping arrangements would be now that she had security at her apartment and her car back. Although they hadn't armed the security system yet since she still hadn't picked all her codes and safe words. But she knew Landon wouldn't leave her until she did.

As for the arrangements, she wanted to know, but the question seemed so forward, especially since she already knew the answer she was hoping for: Landon in her house, and a weekend as lovely and lazy as the morning they'd just had.

She'd almost worked up the nerve to broach the subject when they reached the lot. "That one," she said, pointing to her Corolla, tucked away in a corner under a burned-out street lamp.

But as they drew closer, she got a bad feeling. And since Landon put his arm out to keep her one step behind him, she realized she wasn't the only one. When they were a few feet away, she realized she was walking on glass.

"Streetlight," he whispered. "Someone broke it."

She looked up and realized he was right. The bulb and covering were gone, replaced by remnants, the fallen glass and plastic now crunching under foot.

"Give me your keys."

She did, and he opened the driver's door. The smell got her immediately. A rotting, disgusting smell. Rotten meat spread all over the front of her car and piled into the back seat. And in the summer heat, it was already crawling with maggots.

Her stomach lurched, and she turned away, barely keeping herself from vomiting.

Behind her, Landon slammed the door. A moment later, his arms went around her, and she curled into his arms, her face buried against his chest.

"There was a note, too. Under the wiper blade. It said *Dead Meat.*"

"Oh, God."

"We're reporting this," he said. "No arguments. And you're staying at my place tonight. No arguments there, either."

She nodded, numb.

Gently, he pushed her away from him, then studied her face. "Taylor, baby. Are you okay?"

She shook her head. "No," she whispered. "I'm really not."

Chapter Ten

LANDON GAVE Taylor credit for giving the report to Detective Sanchez without any gaps or obfuscations. Of course, everything she told Sanchez was something that was essentially obvious—the car had been vandalized, she was pretty sure she knew the identity of the perp—but considering how close-mouthed she'd been so far, he'd been afraid she would shut down.

She hadn't, and that was good.

But she still hadn't completely opened up to him, and he was terrified that by keeping her secrets she was hindering his ability to keep her safe.

He slowed to a stop at the intersection of Chicon and Seventh Street, and used that time to glance over at her. Her head was back, her eyes closed, and she kept her hands twisted together in her lap. She was spooked, and he understood that. Who wouldn't be with a restaurant-size supply of meat rotting inside their car? But it hurt more than he liked to admit to know that she didn't yet trust him enough to tell him the whole story.

For most of the drive, he'd been trying to tell himself that he was frustrated because she was making his job harder. And while that was true, it wasn't the problem. No, Landon's frustration wasn't professional, it was personal. He *wanted* her to trust him.

Hell, he just wanted her.

Most of all, he wanted her safe. And now that Beau was escalating his torments, Landon was becoming more and more afraid.

And determined. He'd nail the son-of-a-bitch to the wall, but he needed Taylor's help to do that. Her trust. But damned if she wasn't just like Vanessa had been.

Fuck.

He turned left on Chicon, irritated that his ex-wife had popped into his head for even a second. She was history, and that was a good thing. After five years without her, he rarely even thought of her anymore. She'd been fascinated by his job, but it had also been an albatross. She'd worked in the courthouse and knew the kind of dangers a cop faced. Hell, she'd married him with full awareness of what he did and that he loved his job.

But as the first year of their marriage progressed, she became more and more clingy. They'd fight almost every day when he left the house for his shift. And by six months into their marriage, she'd transferred her fear from him to herself, convinced that the evil he fought on the streets would come after her.

Maybe it would—probably it wouldn't—but either way, he'd begged her to trust him. To believe that he could keep her safe.

But she'd spiraled down, certain that the weight of the criminal world would bear down on her.

Counseling hadn't helped. Talking hadn't helped.

In the end, they'd both realized that her fears about his inability to protect her from the fallout of his job reflected a more systemic lack of trust that permeated their entire marriage.

He'd needed his wife to believe in him. She'd needed—what? He still didn't know. But they never had the connection. They never had that trust.

It had destroyed them, and after eighteen months, they'd gotten divorced.

Now Taylor didn't trust him either. It was goddamn *deja vu* all over again.

Except it wasn't.

He slowed the car to turn right onto East 16th Street, the frustrated part of his mind calming in response to the voice of reason that had seeped in through the cracks.

No, it wasn't the same. Not really. Hell, not at all.

Vanessa hadn't been willing to trust him to keep her safe from a general fear of the boogeyman. Taylor had a legitimate reason for her fear, and she'd told him enough to identify her stalker and to take steps to keep him away from her.

He didn't know what she was holding back—what she wasn't trusting him with—but he knew enough to know there was real fear backing her silence.

And he knew that she'd already trusted him more in just a few days than Vanessa had in the entire time they'd been together.

Feeling calmer, he turned right into the driveway for his bungalow. It was small—only twelve hundred square feet—but he'd fallen in love with the clean lines and nineteen-thirties design. The neighborhood was only a few miles from where he'd been born. From where he'd escaped. And it felt good to come back with the money to buy. To refurbish. To live in a neighborhood that was coming to life again, this time without gangs filling the neighboring houses and drug deals happening on the corners.

And one of these days, maybe he'd actually finish renovating the place.

He grinned to himself as he turned off the car. When that happened, he might have to move. Because he had to admit, the work was one of his greatest pleasures. Manual labor to relieve stress.

Glancing sideways at Taylor, now asleep in the passenger seat, he felt a pleasant tightness curl inside him. There were other ways to relieve stress. And though she looked incredibly relaxed right now, he had a feeling that after the day she'd had, a glass of wine and some between the sheets stress relief might be exactly the way she'd want to spend the evening.

Gently, he brushed her cheek. "Hey, Sleeping Beauty. We're here."

She stirred, then opened her eyes. For a split second, confusion colored her face, but it was quickly replaced with pleasure. And, he thought, relief.

"You're here." Her smile lit up his heart.

"Where else would I be?"

She shook her head, as if shaking off a thought. "Dream," she said. "I'm still groggy. Is this your place?" She'd turned to look out the window at the facade of his little blue house with the white porch railing and colorful hanging pots of flowers, none of which he could remember the names of, but he'd snagged them at Home Depot simply because they seemed cheerful.

The St. Augustine grass in the front yard was mowed, and a huge pecan tree shaded the driveway. Directly in front of his car was a detached garage, but it was a ramshackle building that he used only as a workshop.

"It's small," he said. "But it's mine."

"It's absolutely charming." She turned to face him. "Can I see inside?"

He laughed. "That's why we're here. Come on."

He circled the car and opened the door for her, then led her up the porch steps. He unlocked and opened the door, then immediately stepped in front of her even as he pulled his weapon.

Son-of-a-bitch!

The side window was smashed, and red liquid was spread all over the newly buffed and restored hardwood floors. Paint, he realized from the smell, and felt a quick shock of relief that it wasn't blood.

And right there in the middle of the paint, he saw the message, drawn with the end of his broom that had been tossed aside at the edge of the spill: *She's Mine.*

SHE'S MINE.

The words rang through Taylor, filling her head, making her dizzy. She wanted to sink to the floor, but Landon ordered her to stay behind him as he checked every room, every closet, every nook and cranny of his house.

It was a darling house, too. Charming and comfortable.

And now it was violated. All because of her.

When they finished checking the place, he sat her at the kitchen table and made her a cup of cocoa. She held the mug in two hands and sipped. It didn't make her feel better. Right then, she didn't feel anything.

"I'm sorry," she whispered.

"You didn't do this," he countered, taking a seat across from her. "And in a way this is good."

She laughed at that, the sound almost hysterical. "Yeah, it's super terrific."

He took her hand, and she held on tight, needing that connection. "It means he's watching. And if he's watching, we can find him. We just have to be looking in the right direction."

"Are we?"

He met her eyes, his hard and determined. "We will be."

"I hate that this—"

"No." His word was firm, and the hand holding hers even more so. "No more thinking like that." He drew a breath. "Come on. We're going to go stay somewhere else."

"Where?"

"Where else does a thirty-six year old man go when he has to vacate his house?" He grinned. "That's right, baby. I'm taking you home to meet the parents."

Chapter Eleven

"YOUR PARENTS ARE AMAZING," Taylor said, after she'd been thoroughly welcomed by Gayle and Harvey Bartlett.

She'd grilled Landon on the way over, making sure there was no way that the trouble that seemed to be following her like Pigpen's dust wouldn't soil their life. He'd assured her that their home was isolated and gated, with excellent security. Moreover, because they'd never formally adopted him, Beau would have to dig deep to find the connection between Landon and the Bartletts.

With that reassurance, she'd let herself relax. And the fact that they'd decided to introduce her as Landon's girlfriend and not as a woman in jeopardy meant that there was no talk about Beau or all the shit he'd pulled. Which had gone a long way to making the evening with the Bartletts relaxed and drama free.

Now, Harvey was mixing drinks at a gorgeous oak bar that filled their first floor game room while Gayle slipped off to the kitchen to put together "just a few things to snack on."

"That means another dinner," Landon said, exchanging a knowing look with his father.

"My Gayle isn't happy unless everyone around her is well-fed."

"That's okay by me," Taylor admitted. She went through phases where she tried to avoid carbs, but mostly she just liked to eat. "Especially after sampling her talent at dinner. That was the best lasagna I've ever had."

"It's her go-to meal for when we have unexpected guests." He winked. "And unexpected doesn't mean unwelcome."

"Thanks again for letting us crash here," Landon said, then launched into their planned story. "I wasn't thinking when I told Taylor she could stay at my place tonight while hers is being fumigated. But since I'd just varnished the floors, that wasn't going to work."

"Are you kidding? You're always welcome. Besides, it might have been weeks before you dropped by to introduce your young lady to us." He flashed a wide smile at Taylor. "And that would have been a shame."

He crossed to her then with a highball glass. "It's an Old Fashioned. My favorite. Too sweet for some, but you tell me if you want something else."

"Thanks. I'm sure I'll love it." She'd had the whiskey-based drink before, and it was one of her favorites. Now, she took a sip with pleasure as she watched Harvey pass Landon his drink.

The two men couldn't be more dissimilar. They were both tall, but Harvey was as pale as Landon was dark. And whereas Landon's body was a solid block of muscle, Harvey seemed to be genetically related to the scarecrow from *The Wizard of Oz*. His skinny limbs weren't the only similarity either. He had unruly hay-colored hair that stuck out in all directions. Not to mention the kind of personality that meant you couldn't help but like the man.

God knew Taylor had liked him instantly.

And if Harvey and Landon were different, Harvey and his wife were definitely proof that opposites attract.

A beautiful black woman in her early sixties, Gayle Bartlett had the kind of curves that rivaled Marilyn Monroe. She moved with such grace she almost seemed to float. And she had the same kind eyes as Landon, though there wasn't the slightest genetic connection between them.

What she and her husband shared, however, was an obvious love for their son along with warm and welcoming personalities.

Between snacks and conversation, the evening passed easily, and by the time the Bartletts said goodnight and headed off to the master suite, Taylor felt completely at home.

"Do you think they'd adopt me?" she asked.

"Then you'd sort of be my sister," Landon said, pulling her into his lap. "I don't think I like that idea." He kissed her then, in what was definitely not a sisterly fashion.

"Mmm. Good point." She leaned against him and sighed. "Thank you for bringing me here. Today wasn't the best. You made it better."

"Come on," he said, standing up with her still curled in his arms. She wrapped her arms around his neck and let him carry her to his bedroom, still decorated as it had been when he was a teen.

"Martial arts. Baseball. Marvel comics," she said, glancing at his walls.

"What can I say? I was a pretty cool kid."

"And an incredible man."

He put her on the bed, then told her to relax. Slowly, he undressed her, and though she tried to touch him, he insisted that she stay perfectly still. "Tonight's about you," he said, then proceeded to caress her bare skin. The touch of his hands—roughened by all the work he'd been doing on his apartment—made her squirm and roused her senses. Silently, she spread her legs, then sighed with pleasure when he took the hint, his fingers teasing and playing with her, making her crave a more intimate touch.

"Please," she murmured, but he said nothing. Instead, he moved between her legs, his body hard above hers. He kissed her mouth, nipping at her lower lip before trailing kisses down, lower and lower, until the muscles of her abdomen were quivering in anticipation and her sex was throbbing with desire.

And then, thank God, his mouth closed over her, his tongue laving her core as she arched up, electricity zipping through her, firing her senses and sending her spiraling over—the speed and intensity of the orgasm completely unexpected.

"Oh, God," she sighed. "I didn't—that was incredible."

He slid up her body, then kissed her gently. "Someone needed some stress relief."

"Mmmm. Someone did." Exhaustion weighed heavily on her. She wanted to return the favor, but she could barely keep her eyes open. It had been such a day.

"It's okay," he murmured. "I've got you."

And since she knew he did, she closed her eyes and let herself fall into the dark.

IT WAS past midnight when Taylor woke with a start, her scream caught in her throat.

The dream had been horrible. Beau finding them. Taking her. Torturing the Bartletts.

And then, while she watched, killing Landon.

What the hell had she brought with her?

She knew better. She knew what Beau was capable of. And she damn sure knew that she should have gotten the hell out of Dodge the moment she'd caught even the slightest whiff that Beau was on her tail.

She hadn't. She'd stayed.

And she was going to bring hell down on so many people she cared about. People she loved.

Loved.

She closed her eyes, Landon's image filling her mind.

Did she love him? Could she after so little time?

She told herself it was impossible, but her heart said otherwise. He'd gotten inside her. Made a place for himself. She wanted him. More than that, she needed him. And if that wasn't love, she wasn't sure what was.

In the end, though, that didn't matter. She wasn't going to put him at risk. Not when she knew how to fix it. To make it all go away.

Quietly, she slipped out of bed. Silent tears streamed down her face as she dressed, then padded from the room.

It was easy to get outside, and she started walking down the long drive to the gate at the end of the property. The lovely limestone house stood on five acres outside of Dripping Springs, a town just southwest of Austin. The property was gated, with excellent security, but she knew that anyone inside could get out without triggering an alarm. That was her plan. Walk out, call an Uber, and get her ass to South Austin to find Dominic.

She glanced at her phone and flipped through

her texts until she reached the one from yesterday. She'd sent it as a precaution. A safety net.

But now it was time to use it.

TAYLOR: *It's E. Are you still in the business?*

Dominic*: I'm in. Talk in person. You remember the address?*

Taylor: *Yes. Will be there if and when.*

SATISFIED, she nodded to herself. She'd see Dominic, he'd help her. And by tomorrow night, she'd be long gone.

No more Landon.

No more friends.

Tears pricked her eyes again as she paused on the path, just a few yards shy of the pedestrian gate.

Was this really the way?

Could she really do this? Leave Landon behind?

More important, did she want to?

The answer filled her head, loud and resolute. *Hell no.*

She froze, her heart pounding wildly. Because that was the real issue, wasn't it? She didn't want to leave. Didn't want to run anymore. She wanted to stay here, with the friends she'd made, living the life she'd built.

She wanted Landon. His friendship. His laughter. His touches.

And, yes, she wanted more. Or at least she wanted the chance for what already existed between them to grow into more.

But she'd never get that chance if she ran away.

And maybe—just maybe—he could help her to end this once and for all.

Slowly, she started to turn around. She was still terrified, but she was more resolved, and one step at a time she started back toward the house.

At first, she watched her feet as she walked, unsure of her footing in the dark. Then she lifted her head and saw something moving in front of her. A shadow.

She froze, and was about to turn and run when she realized it was Landon. Jogging through the night toward her. Moving like a silent shadow over the crushed granite drive until he was right in front of her, his breath coming hard.

"You were leaving," he said. "But now you're not?"

"I'm not. I—I changed my mind."

He studied her face. "Why?"

She drew a breath. "A lot of reasons," she admitted. "But the only one that matters is you."

A slow smile spread across his face. "I like that answer."

"I didn't mean to wake you," she said.

He laughed. "I assumed as much."

"I was going to walk out the gate and keep on going."

His eyes locked on hers. "I assumed that as well."

Her mouth was dry, and she licked her lips. "You came after me."

Gently, he reached out, then traced her lower lip with his thumb. Then he held up his own phone and showed her the little dot that represented her. "I would have come a hell of a lot further than the property line."

"Why?" The question was barely a whisper.

"I think you know why." He stepped closer, and the air between them felt charged with possibility. "Do you trust me?"

"Yes."

"Then don't you think it's time we finally talked?"

There was an ironic twist to her smile. "If by

talk, you mean that it's time for me to come clean, then yeah. It's time. I just—"

"What?"

"Nothing," she said. Because how could she tell him that her greatest fear was that once he knew the truth about her, he'd no longer want her anymore?

Chapter Twelve

THEY DIDN'T GO INSIDE. Instead, they sat on a cushioned swing in the yard, far enough away from the house so as to not be in the glow of any ambient light. The night was moonless, and the dark surrounded them like a blanket as the stars blinked down, distant witnesses to the story she had to tell.

He sat properly, his feet on the ground so that he could push them, making the swing rock in a soothing rhythm. She sat with her back to the armrest and her bare feet on his lap. He rested a hand on her ankle, and she focused on that point of connection. She needed his touch to tell the story, and though she was ready to share, she was also grateful that his face was half-hidden in the shadows of the night. Somehow, it was easier to talk to the dark.

"I never lied," she began. "But I never really told the truth either."

She paused, giving him a chance to comment or ask her a question. He remained silent though, and she understood that was how this would work. She'd tell the story from start to finish. And only then would the floor be his.

After taking a long, deep breath, she began again. "It *is* Beau who's after me, but I really did think for a while that it could be Reggie—I wasn't pulling your chain. But I thought so because of the theater references. And, well, because I knew the alternative, and couldn't believe that after so many years he'd found me."

She cleared her throat. "I'm getting ahead of myself. Anyway, once we talked to Reggie, it was clear that Beau had found me. And when I told you he was a creepy ex, that was mostly true, too. He's definitely creepy. And he's sort of an ex. But not the way you think." She paused, looking into the darkness. "Landon?"

She knew he was being quiet so she could get it all out. But she needed to hear his voice.

Gently, he squeezed the top of her foot. "I'm here, baby. I'm listening. Tell it however makes it easiest."

"He—I—my mother left when I was fifteen. My father abused her. I grew up hearing her cry. Hearing the lash of his belt against her skin." She heard her voice crack and paused to take a deep breath. "But she fought back in her own way. She saved money. From the very first day he hit her, she started hiding money away. And the day she left, she gave me what she'd saved up. Nine thousand, six hundred and fourteen dollars and thirty-seven cents. It was in cash—in a metal lockbox—and she showed me how to pull up the kitchen tile to get to the place where she'd hidden it. Then she left."

"For where?"

"I don't know. And she never came back." Her hands were on her thighs, and now she dug her nails into her legs. That had been the worst part—that her mother had said she'd loved her. But she'd left and hadn't once looked back. As if that stupid cashbox was a substitute for having her mother with her. As if those dollars could magically keep her safe from her father.

She'd learned a lesson though. The words *I love you* didn't mean shit. Her father had said them. Her mother had said them. And even though those two were polar opposites, they'd both been lying when those words left their mouths. Real love wouldn't have allowed her mother to walk away like that.

And as for her father ... well, Dale Tucker wouldn't know love if it bit him on the ass.

"She just left me with him." Her voice was a whisper. "Even though she knew what he'd do. What he was capable of."

"Did he ... hurt you?"

She shook her head, then voiced the word when she remembered that she was lost in the dark. "No. Not like you mean. But he was not a good man. He dealt drugs. He dealt weapons. I'm pretty sure he ran hookers. And he double-crossed his business partner. Not that the business was legitimate."

Memories started flooding back, and she hugged herself, trying to keep them at bay. It was no use. The past rushed up, making her stomach churn as she pulled the pieces out to share with Landon. "It was drug money, and the partner was Beau."

"Go on." She heard the tight edge in his voice and was certain that he believed that Beau had killed her father. But it was so much worse than that.

"My dad—he refused to give the money back. And the truth was that Beau didn't care about the money. He had plenty of money. But he saw an opportunity to get something he did want."

"What?" Landon asked.

"Me." Her voice cracked as she spoke. "He'd always watched me. From the time I was ten years old he'd told my mother that he was going to have a piece of me. And on that day, he told my dad that he could keep the money. So long as my dad gave him me. And my father said yes."

"Taylor, I can't even—"

"I ran," she blurted. "I was barely sixteen, but I took the money myself, along with what my mom had given me, and I ran to Austin." She drew a breath. "There are people—you know—who can fix paperwork. Give you a life. I'd been around my dad long enough to know how to find them. So that's what I did. Little Eulalie Tucker became Taylor D'Angelo. I got a driver's license. I manufactured parents. I enrolled in high school. And I tried so damn hard to kill off that old life."

Warm tears streaked down her cheeks. "That's why I didn't tell you. I've kept that secret for over eight years now. And the money's drug money. And I stole it. I knew it was tainted, and I took it. Worse, I spent some of it. Not much. But I used it to pay for some college. Some other stuff. Mostly, though, I used my mom's money and what I've earned. Most of the stash I still have."

She sucked in a breath of air, then slowly let it out. "So there you go. I'm not the woman you thought I was."

"No," he said softly, her stomach twisting with that horrible word. "You're even more amazing."

"What?" She couldn't possibly have heard him right.

"To go through all that? To survive?"

"But I stole that money."

"I know. Doesn't change my impression of you."

"I—" But that was all she could get out. She'd been living with the secret—the guilt—for so long that to have someone be so matter-of-fact completely threw her off her game.

"I'm not saying you can pull it out of the bank and start running around town buying cars and diamonds. But I am saying that there are a lot of mitigating circumstances involved in what you did. How much money are we talking about, by the way?"

"A hundred and twenty-seven thousand."

"And how much do you have left?"

"A hundred and seventeen thousand. And change. All neat and tidy in a safe deposit box."

He actually laughed. "Almost a decade and you've only spent ten thousand? What on?"

"I told you, I used my mom's money first, and for all the stuff I had to do to get my fake IDs. I never, *never* wanted to touch my father's money. But later, I needed tuition money. And a place to live. And I figured that my dad owed me as much. Hell, even if Beau had taken me, he'd have put me some-place to live."

She flashed a wry smile. "Not that Beau would look at it like that. Or the cops for that matter. *Oh*. I mean … shit."

His soft chuckle filled the air between them and his palm closed more tightly around her ankle. "Forget who you're sitting with?"

"For a bit. Yeah."

"Don't worry. I'm not going to slap my cuffs on you. Not for the money stash, anyway. But I can think of some other uses—ouch!"

"Watch it, mister, or the next kick will be real." She tried to sound stern, but she couldn't hide her relief. "You're really not going to, well, do anything?"

"I'm going to do a lot." He lifted her legs, then shifted them both until he was sitting by the armrest and she was in his lap. For a moment, she studied his face, though without a moon, she could read nothing in his eyes. The night was too dark. And so she simply rested her head on his shoulder and let the cadence of his voice soothe her.

"I'm going to find that bastard, for one thing."

"Good," she murmured, her lids starting to get heavy now that the adrenaline rush had faded.

"I'm going to talk to a lawyer about working out a deal for you to turn what's left of the money over to the Arkansas police in exchange for testimony against Beau and your father."

"My dad's already in prison. I looked him up once. He killed somebody outside of a liquor store. But if it'll keep him behind bars longer, I'll repeat the whole sordid story again."

"The bottom line is that we're going to get you clear."

Tears clogged her throat as she nodded. "Beau trashed your house because of me. And yet here you are, doing everything you can to help me."

He brushed her hair off her face, then gently stroked her cheek. "Well, in case you hadn't noticed, I'm rather fond of you."

"Yeah?"

"Yeah," he said, then kissed her so tenderly that she almost started crying all over again. This time, from joy. Because for the first time, she truly felt like she wasn't alone in this. And that felt just fine.

Chapter Thirteen

FOR THE NEXT FEW DAYS, Landon didn't let her out of his sight.

He told himself it was because he was afraid that she'd get spooked and leave again, but the warm, wonderful truth was that he didn't believe that. So he told himself he was sticking close because he was afraid that Beau would find her on his parents' property.

But that was bullshit, too.

No, the real reason that he stuck like glue wasn't because he feared for her safety, but simply because he was a selfish man who wanted her beside him. He wanted to reach out and touch at his leisure. To hold her close at night. To walk with her, laugh with her. To simply *be* with her.

"She's all I think about," he confessed to his

mom, and Gayle had just laughed. "Landon Ware, I can't believe it. You're finally in love."

Was he?

He thought back to his days—and his nights—with Vanessa. The truth was, with his wife, it had been more about the nights. They'd had decent chemistry—though in retrospect it was nothing compared to the intensity of the connection between him and Taylor—but with Vanessa, it had been almost *all* about the sex.

Thinking back now, he couldn't remember a substantive conversation with Vanessa that didn't involve sex or her fears for her safety and his. With Taylor, in the days they'd been together they'd talked about everything from television shows to home renovations to the process of setting up a fake identity. And sex. Though that subject tended to lead to practical demonstrations instead of intellectual ponderings.

They'd also talked about the situation, and although they were staying at Landon's parents, they'd made daily excursions into Austin, spending time on campus near the drama department and also downtown at The Fix. The idea was to draw Beau out—to reiterate to him that despite his real estate shenanigans, Taylor and Landon were a couple—but there'd been no sign of him for days.

Other reasons for Landon's excursions into downtown Austin were to check in with his friends at the APD—no news there, either—and to arrange a meeting with Easton Wallace, a prominent local attorney who both Taylor and Landon knew from The Fix.

Now, Landon stood in the reception area of Easton's office, frowning as his secretary explained that Easton was traveling, but would be back in the office before the end of the week. With that time-line in hand, Landon scheduled an appointment, asking that Easton please meet them in the back bar area at The Fix.

"Why not his office?" Taylor asked as they rode the elevator back down to the first floor.

"I want us to be as public as possible. Anything to catch his attention."

She frowned, but nodded.

He kissed her forehead right before the elevator doors opened. "Scared?"

Her lips curved into an ironic smile. "Definitely, but I was thinking about all the non-public things I enjoy doing with you. Too bad we have to play out the public side of this charade at all."

Her words lit a fire in him that only got hotter when they'd returned to Dripping Springs, and he'd taken her straight through the house to his old bedroom, then made love to her slowly for most of the afternoon.

Later, as they lay naked in each others arms, Taylor rolled over, then propped herself up, her elbows on his bare chest. "I liked doing nothing with you this afternoon," she murmured, her eyes never leaving his.

He reached up and stroked her silky hair, enjoying the way it trailed over his body now that it was falling loose around her face and wasn't tied back in her usual ponytail. "Me, too," he admitted. Then he grinned. "I could get used to this," he said, repeating the words he'd spoken to her after their first time together.

Only this time when he said it, what he meant was, *I love you.*

UP UNTIL THE moment they actually met with Easton in a quiet corner of the small back bar section of The Fix, Taylor had been terrified by the prospect of revealing all her secrets to anyone other than Landon. But then Easton had arrived wearing an air of cool confidence and trustworthiness as prominently as he wore his perfectly tailored gray suit, and her hesitations evaporated.

She'd officially retained him earlier that day over the phone, and at the same time, he'd suggested that Landon retain him as well, ostensibly so that they could all three freely discuss any legal ramifications of Landon's continuing to help her now that he knew about the stolen drug money.

"Oh, God," she'd said. "He's like aiding and abetting, isn't he?"

Easton had only chuckled and told her that at the moment, his only concern was letting them both speak to him with each other present without waiving the attorney-client privilege. "That means Landon needs to be my client, too," he'd said.

Now at The Fix, he reminded them both that, "Anything you tell me is protected by the privilege. I'm like a vault. So you can tell me anything."

It was the perfect thing to say to calm her nerves. Even more, the fact that he'd taken such care to make sure that Landon could be with her during this key conversation, ensured that Taylor was not only relaxed, but trusted him completely.

She had no idea if Easton knew the law, but he

definitely knew people. And she figured that was half the game.

After that, it was easy to dive in and tell him the same story that she'd told Landon. He let her do most of the talking, only interrupting for clarification before he wrote a note on his yellow legal pad.

When she finally sat back, finished, Easton asked Landon about the results of the search for outstanding warrants.

"Several in Arkansas. Mostly drug related. But I got a text this morning. He's got an outstanding warrant in Louisiana. A murder charge. Apparently the prosecution had an airtight case, but the judge let him out on bail before trial. He skipped."

"You manage to catch him, then you can pretty much guarantee that between the Louisiana and Arkansas warrants, your buddy Beau will be going away for a nice, long time."

"Exactly," Landon said, then reached under the table for her hand and held it tight. "Hopefully so long his sorry face never sees the sky without there being bars or a fence between him and the view."

"Cheers to that," she said, then took a sip of the beer she'd ordered when they'd first arrived.

They moved on to the money next, and Easton's thoughts pretty much tracked what Landon had outlined, only in a lot more detail. Still, the bottom line was that she returned the money, but didn't end up with any dings against her because she'd also testify against him and her father. Not to mention Beau's entire organization.

"What about the money I spent?"

"I'm hoping that they'll consider your testimony valuable enough to call it even," Easton told her. "He shifted his attention to Landon. "No sign of Harkness recently?"

"Nothing, and we've been coming into Austin and being very public together at The Fix and around campus for over a week now."

Easton nodded slowly. "Could be he gave up and went home, but I don't believe it. He's biding his time. And you either wait, or you draw him out."

"Not much luck there," she said. "But I'm not sure what we're supposed to do. Strip naked and frolic on Sixth Street?"

"Maybe something close to that," Landon said.

She thought he was joking, but when she turned to shoot him a *be serious* look, she saw that he was looking through the open doorway into the main bar area ... and right at the stage that hosted the Man of the Month contests.

"Perfect," Easton said, without missing a beat. "Get Megan to include you in the flyer for this week's contest. He'll know exactly where you'll be —and when."

"And if I'm on that stage, then I'm not at Taylor's side."

"Exactly," Easton said.

"Um, hello? Doesn't this plan kind of suck for me?"

But Landon only grinned. "Trust me," he said.

And since she did, she nodded and said the only thing she could. "Okay."

Chapter Fourteen

TAYLOR SAT cross-legged on the bed, her computer on her lap, wearing only plain cotton underwear and one of Landon's APD T-shirts. It was two in the afternoon, and she hadn't brushed her hair yet, much less thought about make-up.

Normally on a Wednesday, she'd be hurrying by now, getting dressed so that she could get to The Fix by five in order to set up with plenty of time before the contest. Tonight, though, she was playing the role of bait. Which was why Mina was once again stepping in as the stage manager—and Taylor was enjoying a lazy afternoon trolling the classified section of *The Hollywood Reporter*, checking out potential LA jobs.

For the last year or so, that had been her favorite mindless occupation—poking around and fantasizing about what sort of job she'd get right out of the gate in New York or LA after she graduated.

Lately, though—as in, post-Landon—she'd been less enthused by the New York and LA listings. Instead, the job postings from the Texas Film Commission seemed suddenly quite fascinating. There was even a job at the company where Mina had recently started working.

And, yeah, she was going to ask her friend for the scoop.

Or, maybe she wasn't.

The simple fact was that her entire perspective on her future had changed. Before, it had just been her, alone in the world even though she was surrounded by friends. Leaving town would be easy.

Now, the thought made her stomach ache. She didn't want to be just Taylor. She wanted to be Landon and Taylor.

Trouble was, she wasn't sure if Landon wanted the same thing.

The attraction between them was real—no doubt about that. And she didn't question that he cared about her. But how far did that go? Until they caught Beau? Until he went back to his day job?

Forever?

Please, let him want forever.

She needed to talk with him—she knew that. But when? Not today. Not when they were trying to catch a guy who probably intended to kill her once he caught and dragged her back to Arkansas. The last thing she wanted was to distract Landon with relationship stuff. He needed to be on-game. He was running the whole operation—all while strutting half-naked across a stage.

So when?

It was a question she didn't find a quick answer for, but when he walked through the door moments later in the jeans he wore so damn well, his shirtless torso damp from a shower, her resolve ratcheted up a thousand-fold.

Tonight.

They'd catch Beau, she'd invite Landon to her apartment to celebrate, they'd have wine and make love, and as he held her close, she'd tell him that she loved him.

Assuming she didn't die of nervousness before then.

"You okay?" He sat on the edge of the bed, his brows drawn in concern.

"Just scared," she said, offering the truth and knowing he'd misunderstand.

He took her hand. "We'll have ten plainclothes officers on site. And we don't have to wait for him to make a move against you. Those warrants are cause. You see him, you signal."

"He may not be there at all," she said.

"It's a possibility, but I'm betting he comes."

She hoped so. They'd walked their legs off delivering three times the normal number of flyers around downtown. "Fingers crossed. And of course I'll be looking. But your view from the stage will be better."

He nodded. "True, but I've only seen photos. You're our best hope since he'll undoubtedly be wearing some sort of disguise. Hard for me to see through, but easier for you."

She swallowed and nodded. He was right. Even after eight years, she'd recognize Beauregard Harkness even if he was disguised. His image was burned onto her soul.

"I asked Reece to move one of the tall cocktail tables near the stage," Landon continued. "You can pretend to be so enamored of my awesomeness that you climb on top of your stool to get a better look."

She grinned. "Like a groupie. Nice."

He reached over and plucked at the shirt. "Looks like you already are."

A wave of mortification swept over her. "I'm sorry. I wanted something oversized, and I just pulled open a drawer. I wasn't thinking, and I——"

He silenced her with a kiss. "I like it."

"Yeah? What exactly?"

He chuckled. "All of it. The way you look in my shirt. And the fact that you're comfortable enough to plow through my stuff."

She bopped him with the small pillow supporting her knee. "There was no plowing. I was very neat."

"I may not wash that shirt for months, you know. Once you take it off, it's going to smell like you. The guys at work will wonder why I'm walking around with a constant hard-on."

"Oh, no. No talk like that. We have to get ready. There's no time for sex."

"There's always time for sex."

She bent forward and kissed him, very slow and with a lot of tongue. "After you win the Mr. August crown."

"Well, hell. Now I have to really try."

"Landon? Your mom said you don't date much since you and Vanessa divorced."

Not surprisingly, his eyes widened at the sudden shift in topic. "My mother talks too much."

"Your mother is amazing." She wished she'd kept her mouth shut. Because she was edging very close to the very territory she'd just told herself she wanted to avoid tonight.

But the question of Vanessa had been bothering her, and dammit, it had just popped out.

He'd mentioned her almost in passing to Taylor one day when they'd taken a picnic basket into Austin's Zilker Park. He'd been matter-of-fact, but she'd sensed real hurt beneath the words. And after talking with Gayle, she feared that he'd pretty much sworn off relationships.

And if he had, what did that mean for the two of them?

"Landon?" she pressed when he stayed quiet.

"Mom's right," he said. "Once bitten, twice shy, I guess. Plus, I'm in a hard profession. Tends to scare off anyone who wants stability. You know, sane people. And anyone who does get caught in the net ultimately tears themselves free and runs far and fast."

She nodded, hating that she understood where he was coming from. And hating even more that his view of the world might be a view that didn't have her on the horizon.

She blinked, aware of the tears filling her eyes.

"It was like that with my mom," she said, as much because it was true as to camouflage her tears. "You're right. People don't stick. Things get hard, and they fail you." She drew a shaky breath. "But I really am sorry about your wife."

He took her hand, then held it to his heart.

"And I'm sorry about your mom. But Taylor, whatever happens with Beau, I'm seeing this through to the end. You can take that to the bank."

She nodded, those damn tears finally spilling down her cheeks.

And still the one big question remained—when exactly was the end? And would they still be together afterwards?

BY SEVEN O'CLOCK, Taylor was a live wire of anticipation, so hyped up that not even the Fizzy Watermelon she was sipping took the edge off her nerves.

By eight o'clock, she was parked at the cocktail table by the stage squeezing Megan's hand so tight she was probably shattering bone.

By eight-thirty, her body had started to feel cold, even though she'd started to sweat. She caught

Landon's eye from where he stood on the stage, having just walked the red carpet as contestant number six. He made a campy silly speech about protecting and serving the community by displaying himself half-naked at the contest, then proceeded to strip off his shirt to a chorus of wolf whistles and applause.

If she'd been paying more attention, she might have been jealous of the high level of female appreciation compared to the previous contestants. As it was, she hardly noticed. All she could focus on was his subtle shake of his head. And her own disappointment reflected on his face. *No sign of Beau.*

By nine, she was so frustrated by Beau's failure to show that she didn't even hear when the emcee announced that Landon was the winner, and it wasn't until Megan shoved her forward that she leaped to her senses and started applauding.

He did the usual bow-taking, then hurried down the stairs to her side.

Immediately, the nearby women surrounded them.

Megan, thank goodness, swooped in, telling everyone to give Mr. August some space, and he'd circulate for autographs and pictures in just a minute.

"Nothing," Landon said to Taylor. "Not even a hint of a sign. Goddammit."

Her lips felt cracked and dry, her entire body cold. She'd been so certain that the nightmare would end tonight. "I can't—I don't want to keep looking over my shoulder."

"He may have left town. Realized we had a bead on him, and gotten himself lost. He knows he's got a stack of warrants following him. He gets caught, he's in a cage."

"Maybe."

He took her hand, then held it tight in his own. "You don't sound convinced."

She exhaled. "It's just that even if he did leave, he'll be back. When does it end, Landon—" Her voice broke, and she felt like a fool. But, dammit, she wanted this to be *over*.

"I know, baby. But we'll—*shit*." He cursed the interruption, then grabbed his ringing phone out of his back pocket. "We were supposed to silence them for the contest, but with a ten man team inside and outside the building, I wanted to be able to get calls."

Now, he frowned at the screen, then lifted the phone to his ear. "Go ahead, Sanchez."

He was silent for a minute, and even in the

noisy bar, Taylor could hear the beating of her heart. *Something was happening.* She didn't know what, though. His face was blank. Or at least it was until he looked at her. Then a wide smile lit his face. "Baby," he said. "We got him."

"*What?*" The squeal broke out of her at the same time she launched herself at him. He caught her and spun her, barely missing one of the speakers.

When he put her back down, she was breathing hard, but deliriously happy. "Tell me."

"The team outside identified him and grabbed him. Smooth as silk. They've already notified Louisiana and Arkansas, and he's currently in a cruiser on the way to a holding cell."

"It's over." She held his arm, because if she didn't, her legs probably couldn't support her weight. "I can't believe it."

He bent to her, his lips brushing her ear. "Let's get out of here and go celebrate."

Laughing, she danced backward. "Oh, no. You have to spend time with your adoring public. And I," she added with a wink, "need time to get ready. My apartment. Come when you've finished here. I'll make sure I'm ready." She stepped closer, then rose up on her toes to kiss him, slow and deep and very thoroughly. "Make sure you're ready, too," she whispered.

She broke away then, blowing him one last kiss before she hurried out the door to a street that was safe. A town that felt like hers again.

She'd loved her days with Landon, but dear God how she'd missed the freedom of not feeling like she was under a microscope.

Since she still didn't have a car, she caught a rideshare home, using the short drive to think about the various pieces of sexy lingerie she owned. Or, maybe she should just meet him naked at the doorway…

She was considering all the possible outcomes of *that* lovely idea when she reached her door and slid her key in, only then remembering that she had a security system that she didn't know how to use. For a second, she hesitated, then recalled that she was supposed to have come back with Landon so that they could arm the system and he could make sure she knew all of its features.

Which meant the place hadn't been locked down. *But,* she thought gleefully, that didn't matter since the supreme asshole jerkwad of her life was on his way to a long and fruitful life in prison, where she hoped he'd enjoy his new status as the butt-monkey of someone named Brutus.

With that happy thought dancing in her head, she opened her door and stepped inside—then screamed so loud it felt like she'd ripped her vocal cords as Beauregard Harkness grabbed her by the ponytail, slid the cold blade of a knife against her throat, and whispered, "Hey there, little girl. Bet you missed me, huh?"

Chapter Fifteen

THERE WAS no doubt that the women gathered around him begging for selfies were good for his ego, but after fifteen minutes, Landon had his fill of the adulation. He wanted Taylor, and only Taylor. He wanted to hold her, touch her.

And, yes, he wanted to tell her he loved her. Something his mother had realized even before he had. But Gayle Bartlett was a smart woman, and she knew her son. Because he was head-over-heels. And the sooner he told her—the sooner he learned if she felt the same—then the sooner their life together could begin.

Brent came up to him and slapped him congenially on the back. "Congrats. Couldn't have happened to a better man."

Landon chuckled. "Be careful what you say. You

know you're not getting out of playing this game, right? Eventually, either Jenna or Megan's going to talk you into standing exactly where I'm standing now."

"But until then, I'm the one wearing a shirt."

Landon rolled his eyes and grabbed his shirt off the stage. He was pulling it on when his phone rang, and he missed the damn call. As soon as the shirt was over his head, he pulled his phone out, then frowned when he saw that it was Sanchez. He was about to hit the number to call the detective back, when the phone rang again.

He answered it, an icy dread curling through him.

"Christ, Ware," Sanchez said. "I just got word. It's so fucked up. There was a wreck. Hell, almost half an hour ago, and—"

"Beauregard Harkness," Landon's voice was as taut as a wire. "Where the fuck is Harkness?"

"That's just it," Sanchez said. "We don't know."

———

LANDON SPRINTED FOR THE DOOR, Brent right beside him. "Call dispatch," Landon barked. "Get hostage rescue to her apartment. Hell, get the whole goddamn department there. I'm going to call Taylor. Maybe we got lucky and she hit the grocery store on her way home."

"Already on it," Brent said. "*Go.*"

Landon went, ordering Siri to dial Taylor's number, and praying that she hadn't gone straight home. That she'd gone to buy wine. Cheese. Something slinky to wear. Anything to keep her away from that apartment.

No answer.

Fuck.

His car was equipped with a dashboard light, and he activated it the instant he got in the car. But the damn thing couldn't clear a complete cluster-fuck of a jam, and he ended up waiting through two lights as he edged forward, squeezing in as the logjam of cars maneuvered enough to let him squeeze through.

Three more attempts to call. Three more rolls to voicemail.

He pounded on the steering wheel so hard he bruised his hand.

When he'd finally inched the car forward until he was so close he could almost smell the clear path ahead, he found himself blocked again. He spat out a fresh string of curses, then remembered the tracking app. If nothing else he could at least check her location. And maybe, just maybe, that would prove that she was safe.

He opened the app, hit the button, then waited for his phone to locate hers.

Nothing.

And then—

Fuck.

Her apartment. As big as life on his screen. And she wasn't answering her phone. And he was stuck in goddamn traffic.

Motherfucker.

He abandoned the car, sprinted into the intersection, lifted his badge, and flagged down the first car. A college-aged male in a sports jersey who looked scared shitless. "I need a favor. About a mile that way. As fast as you can. Understand?"

Now the kid nodded, looking scared and excited.

"*Go.*"

The kid went, hauling ass, then turning on a dime when Landon ordered him to, and finally screeching to a halt in front of the larger complex that abutted Taylor's tiny one.

"Turn around here," Landon ordered. "Don't go forward. That's an active crime scene. And thank you," he added, as he practically fell out of the car, his gun now drawn as he raced the short distance to Taylor's complex.

He saw Beau the second he turned the corner into the long driveway off which the individual parking spaces were located. The slimy bastard was standing in front of the trunk of an ancient Chevy —presumably stolen—and was about to slam the hood.

Landon caught a flash of movement and felt sick—the bastard had put her in the trunk. But if she was moving, she was alive.

"*Freeze, Harkness,*" he called, as Beau turned just enough so that he could look back at Landon. The trunk was still open, and Beau held one hand over the open space, a large kitchen knife clutched in his meaty paw, its blade pointed down at Taylor.

"You move, the bitch dies. Think I give a shit? I already got her to tell me where she stashed my money. Amazing what hearing your own bones break will do to someone's desire to cooperate."

Bile rose in his throat. "Drop the knife. Step away from the car."

"Yes, sir, Officer." He started to slowly raise his hands, the knife still in one.

Landon watched, his finger ready on the trigger.

He'd kill the fucker in a heartbeat if it came to that —and damn, but he hoped it came to that—but he couldn't do it if the man was truly surrendering.

And then it happened. A swift blur of motion and Beau turned, the knife starting down.

Landon fired at the same time his mind processed what had happened. Taylor had thrust her bound legs up and kicked. And Beau had acted the way he always did—he attacked.

Landon's bullet had caught him on the turn. A chest wound that knocked him back against the car, then had him rolling to the ground into a pool of his own blood.

Landon didn't even realize he'd started racing for the car until he was already there.

He glanced in the trunk, saw Taylor's sickly twisted arm and her bound body. But she was alive and she wasn't bleeding. She nodded, unable to speak behind the gag. He carefully untied it, then crouched to check Beau.

No pulse. No respiration.

The bastard was dead.

In the distance, he heard the approaching sirens. He closed his eyes and took a moment—that had been too damn close. Then he stood and untied her legs. "I'm leaving the arm tied, baby," he said

163

gently. "I don't want to touch that until you're with a doctor."

She nodded, her face a mass of rising bruises. "I knew you'd come." Her voice emerged soft and gravelly. "Some wild police action totally trumps horny women drooling over you."

He laughed. A real laugh. "God, I love you," he said.

"I know," she whispered, her eyes bright with meaning. "I love you, too."

Chapter Sixteen

TAYLOR SIGHED as Landon carried her into her apartment, careful of her broken arm that, for reasons she couldn't remember, they'd had to cast in old-fashioned plaster. Even after the horror of the last time she was here, it was nice to be home after two full days in the hospital.

He took her into the bedroom, then put her down gently on the bed before sitting gingerly beside her. "What can I get you?"

"You're here. What else do I need?"

He took her hand, one of the few body parts that wasn't bruised. Beau had beat the shit out of her, then broken her arm by twisting it behind her back. The pain had almost been unbearable, but she'd been able to stand it because she knew that for every moment he tortured her, that was another moment of time for Landon to come closer.

She'd never doubted he was coming. And in those long, horrible stretches with Beau, she also knew that being with Landon was the only thing that mattered. Any debate left in her head about where to live had completely vanished. The only place she wanted to be was with him.

And when he'd said those three little words to her, she knew what it was she was surviving for—*them*.

"In that case, there's something I need to tell you."

Her smile hurt, but was worth it. "More than that you love me?"

"I'll tell you that as much as you want. And that's part of it. I want us, Taylor. And I hope you do, too."

She nodded, then saw the relief in his eyes.

"I know you want the Hollywood thing. Or New York. What theater grad doesn't? And I just want you to know we can make that work. I can do private security. I have contacts in both places. So don't think that you have to be tied to where I am. I can move. For you, I'm happy to move."

"But you love your job."

He nodded. "I love you more."

Her body felt light with happiness. "Well, I guess we have that in common." She lifted the side of her mouth that didn't hurt into a smile. "But I don't want New York or LA."

"But—"

"I did," she continued. "But I changed my mind."

He cocked his head as if he didn't believe her.

"Really," she said. "And not just because you love your job here. It's because I love my life here. Our friends. Your cute little house. Your parents. I never expected when I became Taylor that I'd grow roots here, but I have. I don't want to be Eulalie again. I don't want to start over. Not now, anyway. Especially when Austin has tons of film and television opportunities."

He was studying her face. "You mean that."

It was a statement, not a question, but she nodded anyway. "I'd been thinking about it before Beau did his horror movie routine on me. But that solidified it, you know?"

"Yeah," he said. "I definitely do."

"If we want to be coastal later, we can. But we can make the decision together."

"Have I mentioned that I love you?" he asked.

"I think I heard something along those lines." She flashed a quick, pained smile. "But feel free to repeat it as often as you want."

With a sigh, she leaned her head back and closed her eyes.

"Tired?"

She nodded. "And achy." She opened one eye. "I think there's only one place on me that's not bruised—and thank God for that." She shuddered at the thought of Beau touching her sexually. "But I'm in no condition to take advantage of it."

"Oh, I don't know," he said, his tone full of mischief as his fingers went to the tie of the over-sized sweatpants she'd put on to travel home from the hospital.

"Landon," she protested. "I can't … you know … do anything for you."

He had her half-naked now, and he moved between her thighs, looking both sexy and devious. "That's okay. We have our whole lives for me to collect a rain check. Besides, I really want to taste you. So close your eyes and let me help you relax, baby. I promise, my turn will come."

She really didn't have the strength—or for that matter, the desire—to argue. So she did as he said and closed her eyes, letting herself float as his mouth danced over her skin, and his clever tongue teased and tasted, and lifted her up to the heavens.

He was right, she thought, as the pressure inside her built. As the aches and pains fell away under the rising pleasure. They had their whole lives together to make love.

And as soon as she was well, she intended to get right on that.

Epilogue

THE LAST THING Easton wanted after his unexpected night of debauchery and sin was to be mingling at one of the many charity balls that served a dual function as a political mating ground, hooking up potential candidates with potential endorsements with as much efficiency as a finger swipe on Tinder.

And considering he could barely walk straight today, he wanted to be here even less.

Still, he was his firm's golden boy—the man they were trotting out and endorsing as their candidate, and with the firm's power behind him, it would be a huge red mark against him if he didn't manage to bring in at least three more stellar endorsements in the next few months. Ideally with significant funds behind them.

Which meant that despite the fact that Selma had essentially rode him to the moon and wrung him dry, he was at this party to work.

He drew a breath, straightened his tie, and stepped into the chaos of the ballroom. Immediately, a waitress handed him a glass of bourbon, and he took a sip, impressed by the smooth taste with just enough burn to make it worth drinking. He looked up, intending to ask her what label the whiskey was, but instead he froze. Because there she was on the other side of the ballroom.

In a sea of business suits and conservative dresses, Selma Herrington stood out like a sexy sore thumb. She wore skintight leather black pants paired with a black knit tank top. A red belt accentuated her small waist, and her legs seemed all the longer in her four inch heels. She wore a retro style bullet bra underneath the top, a look that some modern men probably didn't care for, but that he thought was erotic as hell, a fact proven out by the tightening in his balls, both from the sight of her and the memory of how she looked last night in nothing but that bra, stockings, and a garter belt.

Her lips were painted fire engine red and her short, spiky hair was tipped with pink and green.

She looked sexy as hell, wild as a forest fire, and completely out of place.

She was also heading straight for him.

"Hello, lover," she purred as she approached.

"Christ, Selma, keep your voice down."

"I enjoyed last night."

He swallowed. "So did I."

Her smile was smug. "I know."

"Why are you here?"

Her brows rose, but he wasn't sure if she was offended or amused. "That's my whiskey you're drinking." She nodded toward his glass. He should have known, of course. She owned one of Austin's fastest growing distilleries. Which was, in fact, part of the reason they'd been together last night.

"Listen, Selma, I need to mingle. I'm going to be announcing my——"

"Meet me in the ladies' lounge in fifteen."

He blinked at her. "What?"

She leaned closer and, thankfully, lowered her voice. "I just have this feeling that you've never fucked in the ladies room during a party. I assumed it was on your bucket list."

"Selma…"

"I want your cock in my mouth," she said, and

he almost groaned aloud. "Or anywhere else you want to put it."

Oh, dear Lord, he was done for.

"Selma, stop. You know I can't."

She lifted a shoulder. "You'd be amazed how much you can do if you just step outside your box. Your box is pretty tight, Easton. I'm just trying to help you push back those walls." She stepped away, then blew him a kiss. "I'll be there in fifteen. Hopefully you will be, too."

"Don't bet the ranch," he said. But as he looked around the mind numbingly dull party ... as his mind started to imagine the sight of Selma on her knees as he fucked her mouth ...

Oh, God.

He wouldn't go.

He couldn't.

But a small part of him damn sure wanted to.

Are you eager to learn which Man of the Month book features which sexy hero? Here's a handy list!

Down On Me - meet Reece
Hold On Tight - meet Spencer
Need You Now - meet Cameron
Start Me Up - meet Nolan
Get It On - meet Tyree
In Your Eyes - meet Parker
Turn Me On - meet Derek
Shake It Up - meet Landon
All Night Long - meet Easton
In Too Deep - meet Matthew
Light My Fire - meet Griffin
Walk The Line - meet Brent

&

Bar Bites: A Man of the Month Cookbook

Down On Me excerpt

Did you miss book one in the Man of the Month series? Here's an excerpt from Down On Me!

Chapter One

Reece Walker ran his palms over the slick, soapy ass of the woman in his arms and knew that he was going straight to hell.

Not because he'd slept with a woman he barely knew. Not because he'd enticed her into bed with a series of well-timed bourbons and particularly inventive half-truths. Not even because he'd lied to his best friend Brent about why Reece couldn't drive with him to the airport to pick up Jenna, the third player in their trifecta of lifelong friendship.

No, Reece was staring at the fiery pit because he

was a lame, horny asshole without the balls to tell the naked beauty standing in the shower with him that she wasn't the woman he'd been thinking about for the last four hours.

And if that wasn't one of the pathways to hell, it damn sure ought to be.

He let out a sigh of frustration, and Megan tilted her head, one eyebrow rising in question as she slid her hand down to stroke his cock, which was demonstrating no guilt whatsoever about the whole going to hell issue. "Am I boring you?"

"Hardly." That, at least, was the truth. He felt like a prick, yes. But he was a well-satisfied one. "I was just thinking that you're beautiful."

She smiled, looking both shy and pleased—and Reece felt even more like a heel. What the devil was wrong with him? She *was* beautiful. And hot and funny and easy to talk to. Not to mention good in bed.

But she wasn't Jenna, which was a ridiculous comparison. Because Megan qualified as fair game, whereas Jenna was one of his two best friends. She trusted him. Loved him. And despite the way his cock perked up at the thought of doing all sorts of delicious things with her in bed, Reece knew damn well that would never happen. No way was he risking their friendship. Besides, Jenna didn't love him like that. Never had, never would.

And that—plus about a billion more reasons—meant that Jenna was entirely off-limits.

Too bad his vivid imagination hadn't yet gotten the memo.

Fuck it.

He tightened his grip, squeezing Megan's perfect rear. "Forget the shower," he murmured. "I'm taking you back to bed." He needed this. Wild. Hot. Demanding. And dirty enough to keep him from thinking.

Hell, he'd scorch the earth if that's what it took to burn Jenna from his mind—and he'd leave Megan limp, whimpering, and very, very satisfied. His guilt. Her pleasure. At least it would be a win for one of them.

And who knows? Maybe he'd manage to fuck the fantasies of his best friend right out of his head.

It didn't work.

Reece sprawled on his back, eyes closed, as Megan's gentle fingers traced the intricate outline of the tattoos inked across his pecs and down his arms. Her touch was warm and tender, in stark contrast to the way he'd just fucked her—a little too wild, a little too hard, as if he were fighting a battle, not making love.

Well, that was true, wasn't it?

But it was a battle he'd lost. Victory would have brought oblivion. Yet here he was, a naked woman beside him, and his thoughts still on Jenna, as wild and intense and impossible as they'd been since that night eight months ago when the earth had shifted beneath him, and he'd let himself look at her as a woman and not as a friend.

One breathtaking, transformative night, and Jenna didn't even realize it. And he'd be damned if he'd ever let her figure it out.

Beside him, Megan continued her exploration, one fingertip tracing the outline of a star. "No names? No wife or girlfriend's initials hidden in the design?"

He turned his head sharply, and she burst out laughing.

"Oh, don't look at me like that." She pulled the sheet up to cover her breasts as she rose to her knees beside him. "I'm just making conversation. No hidden agenda at all. Believe me, the last thing I'm interested in is a relationship." She scooted away, then sat on the edge of the bed, giving him an enticing view of her bare back. "I don't even do overnights."

As if to prove her point, she bent over, grabbed her bra off the floor, and started getting dressed.

"Then that's one more thing we have in common." He pushed himself up, rested his back against the headboard, and enjoyed the view as she wiggled into her jeans.

"Good," she said, with such force that he knew she meant it, and for a moment he wondered what had soured her on relationships.

As for himself, he hadn't soured so much as fizzled. He'd had a few serious girlfriends over the years, but it never worked out. No matter how good it started, invariably the relationship crumbled. Eventually, he had to acknowledge that he simply wasn't relationship material. But that didn't mean he was a monk, the last eight months notwithstanding.

She put on her blouse and glanced around, then slipped her feet into her shoes. Taking the hint, he got up and pulled on his jeans and T-shirt. "Yes?" he asked, noticing the way she was eying him speculatively.

"The truth is, I was starting to think you might be in a relationship."

"What? Why?"

She shrugged. "You were so quiet there for a while, I wondered if maybe I'd misjudged you. I thought you might be married and feeling guilty."

Guilty.

The word rattled around in his head, and he groaned. "Yeah, you could say that."

"Oh, *hell.* Seriously?"

"No," he said hurriedly. "Not that. I'm not cheating on my non-existent wife. I wouldn't. Not ever." Not in small part because Reece wouldn't ever have a wife since he thought the institution of marriage was a crock, but he didn't see the need to explain that to Megan.

"But as for guilt?" he continued. "Yeah, tonight I've got that in spades."

She relaxed slightly. "Hmm. Well, sorry about the guilt, but I'm glad about the rest. I have rules, and I consider myself a good judge of character. It makes me cranky when I'm wrong."

"Wouldn't want to make you cranky."

"Oh, you really wouldn't. I can be a total bitch." She sat on the edge of the bed and watched as he tugged on his boots. "But if you're not hiding a wife in your attic, what are you feeling guilty about? I assure you, if it has anything to do with my satisfaction, you needn't feel guilty at all." She flashed a mischievous grin, and he couldn't help but smile back. He hadn't invited a woman into his bed for eight long months. At least he'd had the good fortune to pick one he actually liked.

"It's just that I'm a crappy friend," he admitted.

"I doubt that's true."

"Oh, it is," he assured her as he tucked his wallet into his back pocket. The irony, of course, was that as far as Jenna knew, he was an excellent friend. The best. One of her two pseudo-brothers with whom she'd sworn a blood oath the summer after sixth grade, almost twenty years ago.

From Jenna's perspective, Reece was at least as good as Brent, even if the latter scored bonus points because he was picking Jenna up at the airport while Reece was trying to fuck his personal demons into oblivion. Trying anything, in fact, that would exorcise the memory of how she'd clung to him that night, her curves enticing and her breath intoxicating, and not just because of the scent of too much alcohol.

She'd trusted him to be the white knight, her noble rescuer, and all he'd been able to think about was the feel of her body, soft and warm against his, as he carried her up the stairs to her apartment.

A wild craving had hit him that night, like a tidal wave of emotion crashing over him, washing away the outer shell of friendship and leaving nothing but raw desire and a longing so potent it nearly brought him to his knees.

It had taken all his strength to keep his distance when the only thing he'd wanted was to cover every inch of her naked body with kisses. To stroke her skin and watch her writhe with pleasure.

He'd won a hard-fought battle when he reined in his desire that night. But his victory wasn't without its wounds. She'd pierced his heart when she'd drifted to sleep in his arms, whispering that she loved him—and he knew that she meant it only as a friend.

More than that, he knew that he was the biggest asshole to ever walk the earth.

Thankfully, Jenna remembered nothing of that night. The liquor had stolen her memories, leaving her with a monster hangover, and him with a Jenna-shaped hole in his heart.

"Well?" Megan pressed. "Are you going to tell me? Or do I have to guess?"

"I blew off a friend."

"Yeah? That probably won't score you points in the Friend of the Year competition, but it doesn't sound too dire. Unless you were the best man and blew off the wedding? Left someone stranded at the side of the road somewhere in West Texas? Or promised to feed their cat and totally forgot? Oh, God. Please tell me you didn't kill Fluffy."

He bit back a laugh, feeling slightly better. "A friend came in tonight, and I feel like a complete shit for not meeting her plane."

"Well, there are taxis. And I assume she's an adult?"

"She is, and another friend is there to pick her up."

"I see," she said, and the way she slowly nodded suggested that she saw too much. "I'm guessing that *friend* means *girlfriend?* Or, no. You wouldn't do that. So she must be an ex."

"Really not," he assured her. "Just a friend. Life-long, since sixth grade."

"Oh, I get it. Longtime friend. High expecta-tions. She's going to be pissed."

"Nah. She's cool. Besides, she knows I usually work nights."

"Then what's the problem?"

He ran his hand over his shaved head, the bristles from the day's growth like sandpaper against his palm. "Hell if I know," he lied, then forced a smile, because whether his problem was guilt or lust or just plain stupidity, she hardly deserved to be on the receiving end of his bullshit.

He rattled his car keys. "How about I buy you one last drink before I take you home?"

"You're sure you don't mind a working drink?" Reece asked as he helped Megan out of his cherished baby blue vintage Chevy pickup. "Normally I wouldn't take you to my job, but we just hired a new bar back, and I want to see how it's going."

He'd snagged one of the coveted parking spots on Sixth Street, about a block down from The Fix, and he glanced automatically toward the bar, the glow from the windows relaxing him. He didn't own the place, but it was like a second home to him and had been for one hell of a long time.

"There's a new guy in training, and you're not there? I thought you told me you were the manager?"

"I did, and I am, but Tyree's there. The owner, I mean. He's always on site when someone new is starting. Says it's his job, not mine. Besides, Sunday's my day off, and Tyree's a stickler for keeping to the schedule."

"Okay, but why are you going then?"

"Honestly? The new guy's my cousin. He'll probably give me shit for checking in on him, but old habits die hard." Michael had been almost four when Vincent died, and the loss of his dad hit him hard. At sixteen, Reece had tried to be stoic, but Uncle Vincent had been like a second father to him, and he'd always thought of Mike as more brother than cousin. Either way, from that day on, he'd made it his job to watch out for the kid.

"Nah, he'll appreciate it," Megan said. "I've got a little sister, and she gripes when I check up on her, but it's all for show. She likes knowing I have her back. And as for getting a drink where you work, I don't mind at all."

As a general rule, late nights on Sunday were dead, both in the bar and on Sixth Street, the popular downtown Austin street that had been a focal point of the city's nightlife for decades. Tonight was no exception. At half-past one in the morning, the street was mostly deserted. Just a few cars moving slowly, their headlights shining toward the west, and a smattering of couples, stumbling and laughing. Probably tourists on their way back to one of the downtown hotels.

It was late April, though, and the spring weather was drawing both locals and tourists. Soon, the area—and the bar—would be bursting at the seams. Even on a slow Sunday night.

Situated just a few blocks down from Congress Avenue, the main downtown artery, The Fix on Sixth attracted a healthy mix of tourists and locals. The bar had existed in one form or another for decades, becoming a local staple, albeit one that had been falling deeper and deeper into disrepair until Tyree had bought the place six years ago and started it on much-needed life support.

"You've never been here before?" Reece asked as he paused in front of the oak and glass doors etched with the bar's familiar logo.

"I only moved downtown last month. I was in Los Angeles before."

The words hit Reece with unexpected force. Jenna had been in LA, and a wave of both longing and regret crashed over him. He should have gone with Brent. What the hell kind of friend was he, punishing Jenna because he couldn't control his own damn libido?

With effort, he forced the thoughts back. He'd

already beaten that horse to death.

"Come on," he said, sliding one arm around her shoulder and pulling open the door with his other. "You're going to love it."

He led her inside, breathing in the familiar mix of alcohol, southern cooking, and something indiscernible he liked to think of as the scent of a damn good time. As he expected, the place was mostly empty. There was no live music on Sunday nights, and at less than an hour to closing, there were only three customers in the front room.

"Megan, meet Cameron," Reece said, pulling out a stool for her as he nodded to the bartender in introduction. Down the bar, he saw Griffin Draper, a regular, lift his head, his face obscured by his hoodie, but his attention on Megan as she chatted with Cam about the house wines.

Reece nodded hello, but Griffin turned back to his notebook so smoothly and nonchalantly that Reece wondered if maybe he'd just been staring into space, thinking, and hadn't seen Reece or Megan at all. That was probably the case, actually. Griff wrote a popular podcast that had been turned into an even more popular web series, and when he wasn't recording the dialogue, he was usually writing a script.

"So where's Mike? With Tyree?"

Cameron made a face, looking younger than his twenty-four years. "Tyree's gone."

"You're kidding. Did something happen with Mike?" His cousin was a responsible kid. Surely he hadn't somehow screwed up his first day on the job.

"No, Mike's great." Cam slid a Scotch in front of Reece. "Sharp, quick, hard worker. He went off the clock about an hour ago, though. So you just missed him."

"Tyree shortened his shift?"

Cam shrugged. "Guess so. Was he supposed to be on until closing?"

"Yeah." Reece frowned. "He was. Tyree say why he cut him loose?"

"No, but don't sweat it. Your cousin's fitting right in. Probably just because it's Sunday and slow. " He made a face. "And since Tyree followed him out, guess who's closing for the first time alone."

"So you're in the hot seat, huh? " Reece tried to sound casual. He was standing behind Megan's stool, but now he moved to lean against the bar, hoping his casual posture suggested that he wasn't worried at all. He was, but he didn't want Cam to realize it. Tyree didn't leave employees to close on their own. Not until he'd spent weeks training them.

"I told him I want the weekend assistant manager position. I'm guessing this is his way of seeing how I work under pressure."

"Probably," Reece agreed half-heartedly. "What did he say?"

"Honestly, not much. He took a call in the office, told Mike he could head home, then about fifteen minutes later said he needed to take off, too, and that I was the man for the night."

"Trouble?" Megan asked.

"No. Just chatting up my boy," Reece said, surprised at how casual his voice sounded. Because the scenario had trouble printed all over it. He just wasn't sure what kind of trouble.

He focused again on Cam. "What about the waitstaff?" Normally, Tiffany would be in the main bar taking care of the customers who sat at tables. "He didn't send them home, too, did he?"

"Oh, no," Cam said. "Tiffany and Aly are scheduled to be on until closing, and they're in the back with—"

But his last words were drowned out by a high-pitched squeal of "*You're here!*" and Reece looked up to find Jenna Montgomery—the woman he craved —barreling across the room and flinging herself into his arms.

Meet Damien Stark

Only his passion could set her free…

Release Me
Claim Me
Complete Me
Anchor Me
Lost With Me

Meet Damien Stark in Release Me, *book 1 of the wildly sensual series that's left millions of readers breathless …*

Chapter One

A cool ocean breeze caresses my bare shoulders, and I shiver, wishing I'd taken my roommate's advice and brought a shawl with me tonight. I arrived in Los Angeles only four days ago, and I haven't yet adjusted to the concept of summer temperatures changing with the setting of the sun. In Dallas, June is hot, July is hotter, and August is hell.

Not so in California, at least not by the beach. LA Lesson Number One: Always carry a sweater if you'll be out after dark.

Of course, I could leave the balcony and go back inside to the party. Mingle with the millionaires. Chat up the celebrities. Gaze dutifully at the paintings. It is a gala art opening, after all, and my boss brought me here to meet and greet and charm and chat. Not to lust over the panorama that is coming alive in front of me. Bloodred clouds bursting against the pale orange sky. Blue-gray waves shimmering with dappled gold.

I press my hands against the balcony rail and lean forward, drawn to the intense, unreachable beauty of the setting sun. I regret that I didn't bring the battered Nikon I've had since high school. Not that it would have fit in my itty-bitty beaded purse. And a bulky camera bag paired with a little black dress is a big, fat fashion no-no.

But this is my very first Pacific Ocean sunset,

and I'm determined to document the moment. I pull out my iPhone and snap a picture.

"Almost makes the paintings inside seem redundant, doesn't it?" I recognize the throaty, feminine voice and turn to face Evelyn Dodge, retired actress turned agent turned patron of the arts—and my hostess for the evening.

"I'm so sorry. I know I must look like a giddy tourist, but we don't have sunsets like this in Dallas."

"Don't apologize," she says. "I pay for that view every month when I write the mortgage check. It damn well better be spectacular."

I laugh, immediately more at ease.

"Hiding out?"

"Excuse me?"

"You're Carl's new assistant, right?" she asks, referring to my boss of three days.

"Nikki Fairchild."

"I remember now. Nikki from Texas." She looks me up and down, and I wonder if she's disappointed that I don't have big hair and cowboy boots. "So who does he want you to charm?"

"Charm?" I repeat, as if I don't know exactly what she means.

She cocks a single brow. "Honey, the man would

rather walk on burning coals than come to an art show. He's fishing for investors and you're the bait." She makes a rough noise in the back of her throat. "Don't worry. I won't press you to tell me who. And I don't blame you for hiding out. Carl's brilliant, but he's a bit of a prick."

"It's the brilliant part I signed on for," I say, and she barks out a laugh.

The truth is that she's right about me being the bait. "Wear a cocktail dress," Carl had said. "Something flirty."

Seriously? I mean, *Seriously?*

I should have told him to wear his own damn cocktail dress. But I didn't. Because I want this job. I fought to get this job. Carl's company, C-Squared Technologies, successfully launched three web-based products in the last eighteen months. That track record had caught the industry's eye, and Carl had been hailed as a man to watch.

More important from my perspective, that meant he was a man to learn from, and I'd prepared for the job interview with an intensity bordering on obsession. Landing the position had been a huge coup for me. So what if he wanted me to wear something flirty? It was a small price to pay.

Shit.

"I need to get back to being the bait," I say.

"Oh, hell. Now I've gone and made you feel either guilty or self-conscious. Don't be. Let them get liquored up in there first. You catch more flies with alcohol anyway. Trust me. I know."

She's holding a pack of cigarettes, and now she taps one out, then extends the pack to me. I shake my head. I love the smell of tobacco—it reminds me of my grandfather—but actually inhaling the smoke does nothing for me.

"I'm too old and set in my ways to quit," she says. "But God forbid I smoke in my own damn house. I swear, the mob would burn me in effigy. You're not going to start lecturing me on the dangers of secondhand smoke, are you?"

"No," I promise.

"Then how about a light?"

I hold up the itty-bitty purse. "One lipstick, a credit card, my driver's license, and my phone."

"No condom?"

"I didn't think it was that kind of party," I say dryly.

"I knew I liked you." She glances around the balcony. "What the hell kind of party am I throwing if I don't even have one goddamn candle on one goddamn table? Well, fuck it." She puts the unlit cigarette to her mouth and inhales, her eyes closed and her expression rapturous. I can't help but like her. She wears hardly any makeup, in stark contrast to all the other women here tonight, myself included, and her dress is more of a caftan, the batik pattern as interesting as the woman herself.

She's what my mother would call a brassy broad —loud, large, opinionated, and self-confident. My mother would hate her. I think she's awesome.

She drops the unlit cigarette onto the tile and grinds it with the toe of her shoe. Then she signals to one of the catering staff, a girl dressed all in black and carrying a tray of champagne glasses.

The girl fumbles for a minute with the sliding door that opens onto the balcony, and I imagine those flutes tumbling off, breaking against the hard tile, the scattered shards glittering like a wash of diamonds.

I picture myself bending to snatch up a broken stem. I see the raw edge cutting into the soft flesh at the base of my thumb as I squeeze. I watch myself clutching it tighter, drawing strength from the pain, the way some people might try to extract luck from a rabbit's foot.

The fantasy blurs with memory, jarring me with its potency. It's fast and powerful, and a little disturbing because I haven't needed the pain in a long time, and I don't understand why I'm thinking about it now, when I feel steady and in control.

I am fine, I think. *I am fine, I am fine, I am fine.*

"Take one, honey," Evelyn says easily, holding a flute out to me.

I hesitate, searching her face for signs that my mask has slipped and she's caught a glimpse of my rawness. But her face is clear and genial.

"No, don't you argue," she adds, misinterpreting my hesitation. "I bought a dozen cases and I hate to see good alcohol go to waste. Hell no," she adds when the girl tries to hand her a flute. "I hate the stuff. Get me a vodka. Straight up. Chilled. Four olives. Hurry up, now. Do you want me to dry up like a leaf and float away?"

The girl shakes her head, looking a bit like a twitchy, frightened rabbit. Possibly one that had sacrificed his foot for someone else's good luck.

Evelyn's attention returns to me. "So how do you like LA? What have you seen? Where have you been? Have you bought a map of the stars yet? Dear God, tell me you're not getting sucked into all that tourist bullshit."

"Mostly I've seen miles of freeway and the inside of my apartment."

"Well, that's just sad. Makes me even more glad that Carl dragged your skinny ass all the way out here tonight."

I've put on fifteen welcome pounds since the years when my mother monitored every tiny thing that went in my mouth, and while I'm perfectly happy with my size-eight ass, I wouldn't describe it as skinny. I know Evelyn means it as a compliment, though, and so I smile. "I'm glad he brought me, too. The paintings really are amazing."

"Now don't do that—don't you go sliding into the polite-conversation routine. No, no," she says before I can protest. "I'm sure you mean it. Hell, the paintings are wonderful. But you're getting the flat-eyed look of a girl on her best behavior, and we can't have that. Not when I was getting to know the real you."

"Sorry," I say. "I swear I'm not fading away on you."

Because I genuinely like her, I don't tell her that she's wrong—she hasn't met the real Nikki Fairchild. She's met Social Nikki who, much like Malibu Barbie, comes with a complete set of accessories. In my case, it's not a bikini and a convertible. Instead, I have the *Elizabeth Fairchild Guide for Social Gatherings*.

My mother's big on rules. She claims it's her Southern upbringing. In my weaker moments, I agree. Mostly, I just think she's a controlling bitch. Since the first time she took me for tea at the Mansion at Turtle Creek in Dallas at age three, I have had the rules drilled into my head. How to walk, how to talk, how to dress. What to eat, how much to drink, what kinds of jokes to tell.

I have it all down, every trick, every nuance, and I wear my practiced pageant smile like armor against the world. The result being that I don't think I could truly be myself at a party even if my life depended on it.

This, however, is not something Evelyn needs to know.

"Where exactly are you living?" she asks.

"Studio City. I'm sharing a condo with my best friend from high school."

"Straight down the 101 for work and then back home again. No wonder you've only seen concrete. Didn't anyone tell you that you should have taken an apartment on the Westside?"

"Too pricey to go it alone," I admit, and I can tell that my admission surprises her. When I make the effort—like when I'm Social Nikki—I can't help but look like I come from money. Probably because

I do. Come from it, that is. But that doesn't mean I brought it with me.

"How old are you?"

"Twenty-four."

Evelyn nods sagely, as if my age reveals some secret about me. "You'll be wanting a place of your own soon enough. You call me when you do and we'll find you someplace with a view. Not as good as this one, of course, but we can manage something better than a freeway on-ramp."

"It's not that bad, I promise."

"Of course it's not," she says in a tone that says the exact opposite. "As for views," she continues, gesturing toward the now-dark ocean and the sky that's starting to bloom with stars, "you're welcome to come back anytime and share mine."

"I might take you up on that," I admit. "I'd love to bring a decent camera back here and take a shot or two."

"It's an open invitation. I'll provide the wine and you can provide the entertainment. A young woman loose in the city. Will it be a drama? A rom-com? Not a tragedy, I hope. I love a good cry as much as the next woman, but I like you. You need a happy ending."

I tense, but Evelyn doesn't know she's hit a

nerve. That's why I moved to LA, after all. New life. New story. New Nikki.

I ramp up the Social Nikki smile and lift my champagne flute. "To happy endings. And to this amazing party. I think I've kept you from it long enough."

"Bullshit," she says. "I'm the one monopolizing you, and we both know it."

We slip back inside, the buzz of alcohol-fueled conversation replacing the soft calm of the ocean.

"The truth is, I'm a terrible hostess. I do what I want, talk to whoever I want, and if my guests feel slighted they can damn well deal with it."

I gape. I can almost hear my mother's cries of horror all the way from Dallas.

"Besides," she continues, "this party isn't supposed to be about me. I put together this little shindig to introduce Blaine and his art to the community. He's the one who should be doing the mingling, not me. I may be fucking him, but I'm not going to baby him."

Evelyn has completely destroyed my image of how a hostess for the not-to-be-missed social event of the weekend is supposed to behave, and I think I'm a little in love with her for that.

"I haven't met Blaine yet. That's him, right?" I

point to a tall reed of a man. He is bald, but sports a red goatee. I'm pretty sure it's not his natural color. A small crowd hums around him, like bees drawing nectar from a flower. His outfit is certainly as bright as one.

"That's my little center of attention, all right," Evelyn says. "The man of the hour. Talented, isn't he?" Her hand sweeps out to indicate her massive living room. Every wall is covered with paintings. Except for a few benches, whatever furniture was once in the room has been removed and replaced with easels on which more paintings stand.

I suppose technically they are portraits. The models are nudes, but these aren't like anything you would see in a classical art book. There's something edgy about them. Something provocative and raw. I can tell that they are expertly conceived and carried out, and yet they disturb me, as if they reveal more about the person viewing the portrait than about the painter or the model.

As far as I can tell, I'm the only one with that reaction. Certainly the crowd around Blaine is glowing. I can hear the gushing praise from here.

"I picked a winner with that one," Evelyn says. "But let's see. Who do you want to meet? Rip Carrington and Lyle Tarpin? Those two are guaranteed drama, that's for damn sure, and your room-mate will be jealous as hell if you chat them up."

"She will?"

Evelyn's brows arch up. "Rip and Lyle? They've been feuding for weeks." She narrows her eyes at me. "The fiasco about the new season of their sitcom? It's all over the Internet? You really don't know them?"

"Sorry," I say, feeling the need to apologize. "My school schedule was pretty intense. And I'm sure you can imagine what working for Carl is like."

Speaking of …

I glance around, but I don't see my boss anywhere.

"That is one serious gap in your education," Evelyn says. "Culture—and yes, pop culture counts —is just as important as—what did you say you studied?"

"I don't think I mentioned it. But I have a double major in electrical engineering and computer science."

"So you've got brains and beauty. See? That's something else we have in common. Gotta say, though, with an education like that, I don't see why you signed up to be Carl's secretary."

I laugh. "I'm not, I swear. Carl was looking for

someone with tech experience to work with him on the business side of things, and I was looking for a job where I could learn the business side. Get my feet wet. I think he was a little hesitant to hire me at first—my skills definitely lean toward tech—but I convinced him I'm a fast learner."

She peers at me. "I smell ambition."

I lift a shoulder in a casual shrug. "It's Los Angeles. Isn't that what this town is all about?"

"Ha! Carl's lucky he's got you. It'll be interesting to see how long he keeps you. But let's see ... who here would intrigue you ...?"

She casts about the room, finally pointing to a fifty-something man holding court in a corner. "That's Charles Maynard," she says. "I've known Charlie for years. Intimidating as hell until you get to know him. But it's worth it. His clients are either celebrities with name recognition or power brokers with more money than God. Either way, he's got all the best stories."

"He's a lawyer?"

"With Bender, Twain & McGuire. Very prestigious firm."

"I know," I say, happy to show that I'm not entirely ignorant, despite not knowing Rip or Lyle. "One of my closest friends works for the firm. He started here but he's in their New York office now."

"Well, come on, then, Texas. I'll introduce you." We take one step in that direction, but then Evelyn stops me. Maynard has pulled out his phone, and is shouting instructions at someone. I catch a few well-placed curses and eye Evelyn sideways. She looks unconcerned "He's a pussycat at heart. Trust me, I've worked with him before. Back in my agenting days, we put together more celebrity biopic deals for our clients than I can count. And we fought to keep a few tell-alls off the screen, too." She shakes her head, as if reliving those glory days, then pats my arm. "Still, we'll wait 'til he calms down a bit. In the meantime, though ..."

She trails off, and the corners of her mouth turn down in a frown as she scans the room again. "I don't think he's here yet, but—oh! Yes! Now *there's* someone you should meet. And if you want to talk views, the house he's building has one that makes my view look like, well, like yours." She points toward the entrance hall, but all I see are bobbing heads and haute couture. "He hardly ever accepts invitations, but we go way back," she says.

I still can't see who she's talking about, but then the crowd parts and I see the man in profile. Goose bumps rise on my arms, but I'm not cold. In fact, I'm suddenly very, very warm.

He's tall and so handsome that the word is almost an insult. But it's more than that. It's not his looks, it's his *presence*. He commands the room simply by being in it, and I realize that Evelyn and I aren't the only ones looking at him. The entire crowd has noticed his arrival. He must feel the weight of all those eyes, and yet the attention doesn't faze him at all. He smiles at the girl with the champagne, takes a glass, and begins to chat casually with a woman who approaches him, a simpering smile stretched across her face.

"Damn that girl," Evelyn says. "She never did bring me my vodka."

But I barely hear her. "Damien Stark," I say. My voice surprises me. It's little more than breath.

Evelyn's brows rise so high I notice the movement in my peripheral vision. "Well, how about that?" she says knowingly. "Looks like I guessed right."

"You did," I admit. "Mr. Stark is just the man I want to see."

I hope you enjoyed the excerpt! Grab your own copy of Release Me ... or any of the books in the series now!

The Original Trilogy
Release Me

Claim Me

Complete Me

And Beyond...
Anchor Me

Lost With Me

Some rave reviews for J. Kenner's sizzling romances...

I just get sucked into these books and can not get enough of this series. They are so well written and as satisfying as each book is they leave you greedy for more. — Goodreads reviewer on *Wicked Torture*

A sizzling, intoxicating, sexy read!!!! J. Kenner had me devouring Wicked Dirty, the second installment of *Stark World Series* in one sitting. I loved everything about this book from the opening pages to the raw and vulnerable characters. With her sophisticated prose, Kenner created a love story that had the perfect blend of lust, passion, sexual tension, raw emotions and love. - Michelle, Four Chicks Flipping Pages

Wicked Dirty CLAIMED and CONSUMED every ounce of me from the very first page. Mind racing. Pulse pounding. Breaths bated. Feels flowing. Eyes wide in anticipation. Heart beating out of my chest. I felt the current of *Wicked Dirty* flow through me. I was DRUNK on this book that was my fine whiskey, so smooth and spectacular, and could not get enough of this *Wicked Dirty* drink. - Karen Bookalicious Babes Blog

"Sinfully sexy and full of heart. Kenner shines in this second chance, slow burn of a romance. Wicked Grind is the perfect book to kick off your summer."- *K. Bromberg, New York Times bestselling author (on Wicked Grind)*

"J. Kenner never disappoints~her books just get better and better." - *Mom's Guilty Pleasure (on Wicked Grind)*

"I don't think J. Kenner could write a bad story if she tried. ... Wicked Grind is a great beginning to what I'm positive will be a very successful series. ... The line forms here." *iScream Books (On Wicked Grind)*

"Scorching, sweet, and soul-searing, *Anchor Me* is the ultimate love story that stands the test of time and tribulation. THE TRUEST LOVE!" *Bookalicious Babes Blog (on Anchor Me)*

"J. Kenner has brought this couple to life and the character connection that I have to these two holds no bounds and that is testament to J.

Kenner's writing ability." *The Romance Cover (on Anchor Me)*

"J. Kenner writes an emotional and personal story line. ... The premise will captivate your imagination; the characters will break your heart; the romance continues to push the envelope." *The Reading Café (on Anchor Me)*

"Kenner may very well have cornered the market on sinfully attractive, dominant antiheroes and the women who swoon for them . . ." *Romantic Times*

"*Wanted* is another J. Kenner masterpiece . . . This was an intriguing look at self-discovery and forbidden love all wrapped into a neat little action-suspense package. There was plenty of sexual tension and eventually action. Evan was hot, hot, hot! Together, they were combustible. But can we expect anything less from J. Kenner?" *Reading Haven*

"*Wanted* by J. Kenner is the whole package! A toe-curling smokin' hot read, full of incredible characters and a brilliant storyline that you won't be able to get enough of. I can't wait for the next book in this series . . . I'm hooked!" *Flirty & Dirty Book Blog*

"J. Kenner's evocative writing thrillingly captures the power of physical attraction, the pull of longing, the universe-altering effect one person can have on another. . . . *Claim Me* has the emotional depth to back up the sex . . . Every scene is infused with both erotic tension, and the tension of wondering what lies beneath Damien's veneer – and how and when it will be revealed." *Heroes and Heartbreakers*

"*Claim Me* by J. Kenner is an erotic, sexy and exciting ride. The story between Damien and Nikki is amazing and written beautifully. The intimate and detailed sex scenes will leave you fanning yourself to cool down. With the writing style of Ms. Kenner you almost feel like you are there in the story riding along the emotional rollercoaster with Damien and Nikki." *Fresh Fiction*

"PERFECT for fans of *Fifty Shades of Grey* and *Bared to You*. *Release Me* is a powerful and erotic romance novel that is sure to make adult romance readers sweat, sigh and swoon." *Reading, Eating & Dreaming Blog*

"I will admit, I am in the 'I loved *Fifty Shades*' camp,

but after reading *Release Me*, Mr. Grey only scratches the surface compared to Damien Stark." *Cocktails and Books Blog*

"It is not often when a book is so amazingly well-written that I find it hard to even begin to accurately describe it . . . I recommend this book to everyone who is interested in a passionate love story." *Romancebookworm's Reviews*

"The story is one that will rank up with the *Fifty Shades* and Cross Fire trilogies." *Incubus Publishing Blog*

"The plot is complex, the characters engaging, and J. Kenner's passionate writing brings it all perfectly together." *Harlequin Junkie*

Seduce Me

Unwrap Me

Deepest Kiss

Entice Me

Hold Me

Please Me

The Steele Books/Stark International:

He was the only man who made her feel alive.

Say My Name

On My Knees

Under My Skin

Take My Dare (includes short story Steal My Heart)

Stark International Novellas:

Meet Jamie & Ryan-so hot it sizzles.

Tame Me

Tempt Me

S.I.N. Trilogy:

It was wrong for them to be together…

…but harder to stay apart.

Dirtiest Secret

Hottest Mess

Sweetest Taboo

Stand alone novels:

Most Wanted:

Three powerful, dangerous men.

Three sensual, seductive women.

Wanted

Heated

Ignited

Wicked Nights (Stark World):

Sometimes it feels so damn good to be bad.

Wicked Grind

Wicked Dirty

Wicked Torture

Man of the Month

Who's your man of the month …?

Down On Me

Hold On Tight

Need You Now

Start Me Up

Get It On

In Your Eyes

Turn Me On

Shake It Up

All Night Long

In Too Deep

Light My Fire

Walk The Line

Bar Bites: A Man of the Month Cookbook(by J. Kenner
& Suzanne M. Johnson)

Additional Titles

Wild Thing

One Night (A Stark World short story in the Second
Chances anthology)

Also by Julie Kenner

The Protector (Superhero) Series:
The Cat's Fancy (prequel)
Aphrodite's Kiss
Aphrodite's Passion
Aphrodite's Secret
Aphrodite's Flame
Aphrodite's Embrace (novella)
Aphrodite's Delight (novella – free download)

Demon Hunting Soccer Mom Series:
Carpe Demon
California Demon
Demons Are Forever
Deja Demon
The Demon You Know (short story)
Demon Ex Machina

Also by Julie Kenner

Pax Demonica
Day of the Demon

The Dark Pleasures Series:
Caress of Darkness
Find Me In Darkness
Find Me In Pleasure
Find Me In Passion
Caress of Pleasure

The Blood Lily Chronicles:
Tainted
Torn
Turned

Rising Storm:
Rising Storm: Tempest Rising
Rising Storm: Quiet Storm

Devil May Care:
Seducing Sin
Tempting Fate

About the Author

J. Kenner (aka Julie Kenner) is the *New York Times, USA Today, Publishers Weekly, Wall Street Journal* and #1 International bestselling author of over one hundred novels, novellas and short stories in a variety of genres.

JK has been praised by *Publishers Weekly* as an author with a "flair for dialogue and eccentric characterizations" and by *RT Bookclub* for having "cornered the market on sinfully attractive, dominant antiheroes and the women who swoon for them." A six-time finalist for Romance Writers of America's prestigious RITA award, JK took home the first RITA trophy awarded in the category of erotic romance in 2014 for her novel, *Claim Me* (book 2 of her Stark Trilogy).

In her previous career as an attorney, JK worked as a lawyer in Southern California and Texas. She currently lives in Central Texas, with her husband, two daughters, and two rather spastic cats.

More ways to connect:

www.jkenner.com

Text JKenner to 21000 for JK's text alerts.

f facebook.com/jkennerbooks

🐦 twitter.com/juliekenner

87744184R00127

Made in the USA
Lexington, KY
29 April 2018